# THE THINGS THAT ARE LOST

# THE THINGS THAT ARE LOST

Alan Kennedy

LASSERRADE

First published in the United Kingdom in 2018 by Lasserrade Press.

Cover illustration: Pierre-Auguste Renoir (1880), Portrait of
Mademoiselle Irène Cahen d'Anvers ("little Irène"), Sammlung_E.G.

*For Elizabeth*

*Albert Bradley (1881-)*
*"Girl in Straw Hat"*
*signed 'Bradley' (lower right)*
*dated 'Mai 18.' (on the reverse)*
*oil on canvas 342 x 439.2 cm.*

# one


*Saturday June 10 1944*

*Inverness*

HE pulled the jeep into the kerb and killed the engine, suddenly aware he had not the faintest idea what came next.

If this was what escape felt like, the sentiment was overrated - *exhilaration*, wasn't that meant to be the word? And maybe it had been a bit like that, at least at the start, driving too fast, checking the mirror like some demented getaway man.

All gone now: drained away.

Nothing left.

Just the damp silence of Inverness and a curious furtive feeling, wondering what they'd say when he got back.

If he went back.

After all, hadn't somebody once said he was expendable? You never know, perhaps the delinquent boy who'd run away was never meant to go home.

Not that anyone sane would describe *Station 402 Signals Torridon*, as home.


Somebody had left a packet of Players under the dashboard. He shook one out, lighting it, letting a plume of smoke hang thick between his lips, staring into the darkness.

*What the hell came next?*

Deserted blackout Inverness stared back at him, the one visible road a dreary line of cramped stone houses, dissolving at the farther end into a grey pall of coal smoke, everywhere the smell of tar.

Weren't the buggers supposed to be celebrating D-Day? Didn't they know what it cost to bring cheer to their shrivelled Scottish hearts? Obviously, if the news had reached this godforsaken dump, the residents were keeping it to themselves: it was hard to believe this street was ever anything but deserted.

The faint orange glow from the panelled door of the pub flickered like a candle in a church.

The place wore silence like a shroud.

Alex had yet to learn that in Inverness talk is an impediment: the place was crowded, massive soldiers smelling of wet cloth stuffed shoulder to shoulder at the bar, green tooried bonnets adding an air of threatening gaiety to khaki uniforms.

As he came in, a dozen wary eyes fixed him in a huge mirror, gilt letters emblazoned *Dewar's Whisky*. A ripple of soft voices fluttered through the silence.

He ordered brandy, embarrassed at the sound of his own voice, the man behind the bar throwing a sly sidelong smirk at the others, measuring it out.

That had been four drinks ago.

Or was it five?

He had forgotten.

Also forgotten, exactly when she had come in.

He had seen the door open, bringing its whiff of tar, seen someone take the other chair at his table, slowly become aware of a soft highland accent washing over him, a tiny face, sharp features, black hair combed to a severe white line across her scalp.

She seemed a restless soul, forever leaning down to the floor feeling for her bag, hauling it up, fumbling inside for cigarettes.

He caught her eyes as she inched the packet towards him with a fingertip, frowning as he reached mechanically for his case, shaking her head too vehemently as he opened it for her.

Somewhere beyond the sweet taste of brandy some part of him had begun to keep watch, conscious of an inner commentary that at first he did not quite believe.

In all his life, Alex Vere had never picked up a woman, even wondered about the mechanics, how you went about it.

It was something that happened in books.

Justine would have known.


Now and then she would turn aside, head tilted in profile, her tongue flicking fretfully across tiny white teeth, as if she was trying to lick something off.

Watching it come and go he heard the inner lucid voice arguing the toss, weighing the odds.

"Another?"

Smiling, scraping her chair legs back, one hand flapping for her bag.

"You're going it a bit. What is that stuff, anyway?"

"Brandy." Adding, because she seemed offended he had not returned her smile, "Brandy. You know. Artists drink it."

"Those that can afford it, I dare say."

She fished her handbag up, laying it on the table, snapping it closed.

"That what you are? I've never met an artist. That why you're eyeing me? What brings you here? Torridon now, that's miles away."

"*Torridon*. What the hell d'you mean? What ..."

"No need to chop my head off. The jeep. It was always here not so long ago. Nice boys, as well." She glancing across to the bar, dropping her voice: "There was one ... Patrick he said his name was ... lovely boy. He had no uniform, either."

"I'd be careful if I were you."

"If you say so, Mr Artist." She was trying to stare him down, defiant patches of red high on each cheek. "But you've chosen your night, haven't you?"

Reading the look on his face, she jerked her head to the men at the bar. "They're always going on about it. No uniform. It's the look of it, I suppose. Can't say it bothers me ... it's just clothes when it comes to it. That boy with the jeep was English, though … like you. This lot always pick at that if there's nothing else to pick at. But I'm right, aren't I? You're from there. You've that same look. Half starved. You a spy then?"

"Now you know where that sort of talk can land you, don't you?" Alex leaned back, managing a tiny smile to take the sting away.

She started to speak, changing her mind, finally settling to something: "I could if you like ... you know … *pose*. Posing you call it. Not for nothing, mind you."

"No, I'm not an artist. You're mistaken on that score – nothing further from the truth."

He closed his eyes, remembering an indefinite line of dead faces, struggling to remember a Patrick among them. Nothing came, apart from the weary certainty Patrick would be dead by now. It was all they had in common now: they were all dead. Perhaps he should explain that her boy had been shot. Shot if he was lucky: more likely hanged in some French prison cell.

He remembered at last why he had ordered brandy. His last safe time with Justine, lost in the fog of war somewhere in France – some other godforsaken place. The desperate fag end of a failed mission. Dawn had brought them to the safe house against all the odds. He remembered the rain coming on, Justine barely alive. They had been drinking brandy then.

He looked across to the woman's artless upturned face, its baffled expression a little pained, knowing he was too weary to explain. Watched her stand, her skirt too tight, pushing an awkward way through the blue haze to the bar, sharing a joke with someone he could not quite make out.

4

As the man behind the bar filled a tiny metal jug, she leaned across the counter, smiling into his face, hitching one leg up, the seam of her stocking crooked in the hollow of her knee.

Nice legs. Long as well. Long, for someone so small.

She turned to look at him, taking him unawares, her sudden brazen stare scalding him.

Sliding his glass across the table she let a drop jerk out across the back of her hand, licking it away, pulling a face.

"That's fierce stuff, that is," reaching out to touch his arm, "what d'you do, then, if you're not an artist? D'you stay in Inverness? What's your name?"

The smell of brandy fresh on her breath overwhelmed him, squeezing his eyes closed.

*What the hell came next?*

What was he supposed to do?

Take her home to fuck? Was it that she had in mind?

Smuggle her past the sniggering Guard House. *Got your leg over, Sir?*

No, no, impossible. He forgot, Torridon was miles away, no home there. Where then? The two of them tottering through dreary streets to some other home.

Naked, would this tiny body spirit Justine back? What do you do with someone you did not know?

Someone who was not Justine?

He could feel her searching his face, puzzled at his eyes shut-tight, shoving hard against his arm.

"Have you got a name, then?"

Another memory spiralling from nowhere: Justine drawing him close, her hair across his eyes, the sun breaking through pine trees, suddenly hot. Everywhere the bitter scent of wood smoke. Justine resting her lips on his, barely a kiss, two hands behind his head.

He flinched as she prodded him again, hearing his voice as if it was someone else.

"No names, no pack drill. What happened to your pack, anyway? You never said. No … sorry … thinking of someone else. Bit addled. Got you muddled there."

"With your girl? I hear that a lot, you know. Or wife is it? What's she called?"

"No girl. No wife."

"Go on … you say that."

"And it's bloody true."

The man behind the bar stopped polishing a glass, looking across.

"No need to shout. You'll have us chucked out. Donny doesn't like shouting."

"No, you're right. Sorry … sorry. Look, best leave me to myself. Things to think about."

She scraped her chair back, pressing one hand on the table to steady herself.

"Suit yourself, I'm sure." Half standing, changing her mind, slumping back down, bag tight against her knees. "Looks like you'll have to put up with me. There's only here to sit."

She leaned forward, her head touching his, suddenly conspiratorial.

"Sheila, if you're interested. That's my name. I never liked it, but my mother must have. So there you are, Mr Mysterious."

He felt her hand feebly pecking at the cloth of his sleeve.

"D'you want another? That's six of those you've had, mind. He'll be at the bell in a minute."

Eyes closed, Alex reached out, taking her wrist in his hand, feeling bone through the fabric of her coat. Too frail. Everything seemed wrong.

"Yes, get me another Justine. Here … wait … take this ..."

"Sheila. The name's Sheila. You've had too much. He won't take a fiver …"

"Yes he will, Sheila. Get me another, Sheila … if you would."

She dissolved to a blur of creased khaki, staring into small bloodshot eyes, the raw smell of hot beer belching over him.

A beefy man in uniform perched on the edge of her seat, too close, the pom-pom on his bonnet absurdly alien. Why the hell would anyone wear such a thing?

"Go on Shirl, you heard what the wee man said." Clenching an arm round the woman's legs, pulling tight, squeezing skinny thighs. Glasgow accent, hoarse with the smoke, ominously soft.

Alex had known voices like that before. Known too many. These were voices to end your life.

He felt his heart jerk, the throb of something urgent in his neck, a sickening weariness, knowing what came next.

"You heard what he said - he wants another." He pushed the woman away, hands riding up with her skirt. "*If you would.*"

Alex leaned across the table, close enough to feel the heat off the man, knowing already where all this must end.

"Beetle off, will you, there's a good chap. Three's a crowd. She's with me."

"*Good chap* is it? Well I'm no' all that good. An' she's no' your Justine, see?"

"Leave him, Jimmy, you can see how he is. The boy's drunk."

"Oh, aye, he's that. What's he to you?"

"Nothing ... nobody. I dinna know him. And you know Donny won't have it. Not fighting."

"Who's fighting? Away and look for his bevvy." Pulling the five-pound note from her hand, stuffing it in her blouse. "An' you're no' his bloody Justine, mind. Just take a wee minute getting back."

A sudden stink of sweat jerked Alex up, a blotchy face close to his own.

*"Justine*, what sort of name's that, then?"

No one was altogether clear as to what happened next. Except that arms tight round Alex's shoulders fell curiously limp, a kind of animal yelp piercing the room, the scarlet pom-pom joggling back with the soldier's head, an arc of bright blood spinning in the air.

It seemed to Alex that something huge thumped down between them.

But for the spreading stain of red across his face you would have said the soldier slept.

That was when Sheila screamed.

# two

THE interview had been Major Elton's idea, calling across to Alex as they finished dinner in the emptying mess.

He was waiting in his office. Stationed safely behind his desk, back to the window, silhouetted in Scottish sunlight. Uniform a little too crisp.

The dark blue corpse of an Inverness Burgh Police Report lay splayed on the desk in front of him like a sacrifice, its back broken.

Alex burst out laughing.

"You'll never pull this off, Maurice. Honestly, what's it all about? Am I called in for a wigging? The Third Degree? Called to account? For what?"

Elton folded the Report closed, pressing it face down as if to make it disappear, struggling for an authority that had somehow escaped him.

Not long in the job, the last of a succession of passed-over military: the not-quite brigade, the previous one - not long either – having run away to join the real war while there was still some left, anything being better than Torridon's perpetual shadow-boxing. The place had lost its point.

He looked lonely.

A clock ticking somewhere in the room measured out an awkward silence.

"This about Inverness? I don't usually get that drunk, Maurice. Never, really. Look, you don't know me very well, but that's the truth. The situation finally got to me. You're surely not going to ask why?"

Elton turned to gaze through the window to a landscape of black rock, waves of heather not yet in bloom.

"No, I suppose I don't have to."

"It was the news about the landings. I just took things into my own hands. I'm sorry ... that's how it is. Not a hanging offence. Have you any idea how long I've been stuck in this blighted hole, kicking my heels?" Managing a thin smile, Alex tried to soften the petulance in his voice.

"Look, I know it's no defence, but ..."

Elton was already reaching inside a wooden file tray at the head of the desk, scraping out a sheaf of notes in a giant bulldog clip.

"Perhaps we'd better leave *defence* out of it ... complicates things. I'm not accusing ... you realise it's nothing to do with me."

He freed a few sheets from the jaws of the clip, fanning them out.

"Listen to this. Chap on the South Gate. *Captain Vere failed to stop when signalled to do so. Uncertain whether unable or unwilling. Driving erratically.*"

He seemed suddenly embarrassed, "Don't laugh, Alex. It's not bloody funny."

"Oh, I don't know. *Unable or unwilling.* Some of these blokes have a nice literary touch."

"And what if some of these blokes had opened fire?"

"Don't be ridiculous. Old Wrigley wouldn't shoot me. I bought his kid a spitfire last Christmas. Anyway, you know that gate is always open. Not to me, of course, but always open."

Elton changed tack, wriggling round in his chair. "What was wrong with the pub in Torridon? You could have got drunk there if you had to."

"Are you sure? Not on Saturdays I couldn't. Weekdays only, remember? Weekends I need an escort."

"If you'd just waited a couple of days. Couldn't you have done that? You've brought this bloody nonsense down on us all for the sake of a couple of days. It's not as if the place is even going to endure much longer. It's perverse. Look, d'you think you could sit down for a minute."

He opened a cigarette box, pushing it across. "D'you want a smoke? I don't myself. That's why it's full. Came with the desk. Inherited you might say."

He began tapping the Report with his finger, forgetting to stop. "It's alright, Inverness police won't make a fuss about the fight. We're all agreed nothing happened. That's going to be the line."

"Nothing did happen. And it wasn't a fight ... alright, perhaps it was, but I didn't start it. Great big chap, very aggressive. He went for me. What was I supposed to do? I had to defend myself."

"Oh, you managed that alright. If the chaps in the bar hadn't got to him. For God's sake, Alex, you half killed him."

"He was trying to choke me. It's automatic. Once somebody has his hands on your throat ..."

"That's not the point. You turn up out of the blue like that. Peaceful pub ... I suppose it was peaceful, wasn't it? Inverness is always bloody peaceful. You turn up in civvies, the place full of soldiers. I don't want to be rude, Alex, but you look like you couldn't swat a fly. Then what happens? Up you get and fell a great ox of a man. People are going to put two and two together and get five. We have to think about security."

"*Security*? You're joking. You know what some woman in the bar asked me? Whether I was a spy? She'd recognised the jeep. If you think this place is secure ... well ..."

"You didn't have to kill him."

"He was unlucky. It was automatic - the training kicking in. I nearly died that way once when I was operational. It's a lesson you don't forget."

11

Elton stopped tapping the cover, his expression unfathomable.

"I didn't know … not until I looked you up. I didn't appreciate all that." He let the pause run on. "Somebody should have told me. I didn't know. But did you really need to? Perhaps you could have given us a thought."

"When somebody has his hands on your throat, thinking about anything at all is a good way to end up dead."

"Second Camerons, wasn't it? That's a Highland regiment – not given to playing pat-a-cake with civilians. Mind you, brawling in uniform, he'll be in trouble for that."

He pushed the Report away.

"When he recovers, that is. No, the Regiment won't come back at us … at least, probably not. Thinking about it, I don't think we need worry about the fight … or whatever you want to call it …"

They sat in silence on opposite sides of the desk, listening to the tick of the clock. Outside, a low sun stubbornly refused to set, changing the light to a kind of milky opalescence.

Alex crushed his cigarette out, rising to leave.

Elton leaned forward. "Don't go yet, Alex. You're not in a rush, are you? There was something else."

He was struggling with a drawer tight against his stomach, finally pulling something out.

Alex recognised the bulging manila folder. *VERE, A, CAPT.* Faded black stencil, army style.

It seemed to have gained something on its journey to Torridon: a stapled docket on the cover, War Office pink, *SECRET*.

Elton got up to switch the light on at the door, standing with his back to the room, switching it off again, staring out into the gleaming landscape.

"Can't get used to the light here. Never seems to get dark. What time do you make it?"

Alex looked at his watch, "Ten. Your clock's slow."

"I hoped you were going to say why you really ran off like that."

"It's complicated."

"All the same ..." Elton came back to the desk, twisting a feeble circle of light from the lamp down onto the manila folder. "I hadn't realised you were trained here. You must have been one of the first. SOE days, wasn't it?"

"A career cut mercifully short."

"No, Alex, you can't get away with that. What's in here is pretty impressive ... I mean what you did. More than most of us managed. More than me, at any rate."

He had run out of words again, staring down at his finger ends, picking at the edge of the pink docket where it was peeling away, settling his mind to something. He shoved the folder a few inches forward on the desk as if the action might summon up the right words.

"You trained alongside an agent called Justine Perry. No, don't get agitated. She was in that same first crop. No need to say anything. Just so you know I've read this."

"That's more than I have."

"What I mean is, she was the *why* of that peculiar escapade in Inverness, wasn't she? I'm right, aren't I? When they got you tucked away up here, they forgot about Mrs Perry."

"*I* didn't bloody forget about her, if that's what you want to know. I owe Justine Perry my life. I doubt that's written down anywhere. Not a debt you forget, is it?"

"You knew her very well."

"No need to sound so coy. Is it anybody's business? Alright, she and I were ... well it was hardly a secret. Speaking of which, why the docket? Am I going to be told? Or is that a secret?"

"Look, Alex, if you're going to make this difficult." He was shaking his head, irritated, "I'm coming to that."

"I was willing to put up with the situation. All this fake nonsense. I'm used to fakes. I spent a good bit of my time before I was sent up here, faking things. It's not knowing what happened to Justine Perry I can't put up with. That's what's killing me."

"The last time you saw her? When was that?" Elton skipped a beat, knowing the answer. "Can I ask?"

"The day I was posted up here. Dispatched to this place. Good word that - *dispatched*. That was the same day Justine resigned her commission. Since then, nothing at all. She vanished."

Elton had unlaced the folder, extracting a single sheet of paper.

"I've been going through the orders covering your time here."

"That business of keeping me out of harm's way in case I bumped into the wrong man? In case I said the wrong thing? Ridiculous."

"Put it that way if you like. Not my decision. Did you ever see the orders? Anybody ever show you them?"

"Of course not, that would be breaking ranks. I wasn't even supposed to know why I was here. God knows how long they expected to keep that game up. Not that it matters. I do appreciate I'm not that important in the great scheme of things."

"Oh, important enough, Alex. In fact, I don't think you appreciate how important. When I got here they flew a chap up from London just to brief me about Captain Alex Vere. Baker Street I assume – they never tell you." He waved a page of War Office notepaper. "Brought this letter with him. The last CO had exactly the same."

"Written orders about me? It's mad."

Elton didn't reply, anxiously searching for the right words, floundering. He seemed inexplicably embarrassed. "Actually, it wasn't all written ... one bit wasn't. I was told to deal with the situation as best I could. That's what he said."

He looked up, searching for Alex's eyes like a dog in pain. "And I did, Alex, you know I did. Can't say I liked it, but at least give me credit for that."

"Oh, I absolve you, old man, if that's your concern. You mean this business of keeping me away from the natives without the use of chains? By the way, is that how I qualify for a pink tag? I'm impressed."

"I'll read you the orders if you like. Can't see it matters now. This bit: *Captain Vere must be kept on site as far as is practicable.*"

He let the paper drop onto the desk.

Alex stared back at him: "Leaving me to my increasingly pointless lectures. Explaining to a diminishing band of agents how lies work. When best to tell them. You can't say I'm short of experience on the subject. Mind you, the one thing the new crop of agents can't cope with is cynicism, I suppose we should find that encouraging."

"Didn't my predecessor extract some kind of promise from you?" He was scrabbling among a pile of papers, "He left me a note ... can't lay hands on it. Something about excursions. Sounded a bit vague. You know, all nods and winks. But I thought you went along with it."

"You mean that business about parole? I forget his name. Colonel somebody or other. We were quite an important setup then. The final posting for SOE. We were the top dressing. What we were doing was important."

"It still is, Alex."

"If you say so. The good Colonel condescended to see me exactly once."

Elton was still turning pages, still looking, "But you did go along with it?"

"Not because he asked me. It was barmy. Started quoting Geneva Article 21 at me. Asked whether I was willing to be honour bound not to stray, in the interests of operational security. I remember I asked him whether he was aware the Geneva Convention related to prisoners of war. He got shirty and said he only meant it by way of example."

"That's not the point, Alex. You realise this place doesn't exist, don't you? I mean Station 402. Surely you see that puts you in rather a peculiar position?"

"You mean ergo Captain Vere hasn't existed for the past year or more, either? Well, he can put up with that. Set your mind at rest on that score."

Watching Elton fidgeting with the folder, Alex leaned forward.

"I suppose there's no point my asking who signed these famous orders?"

"They came right from the top, believe me. War Cabinet Office. All a bit heavy handed."

"But the name. Can't you tell me? I've been kept under a kind of house arrest for months on the say-so of somebody ..."

"All signed off, Alex. There's no point ..."

"Oh, I'm not questioning the legality. I'm not that stupid. But it would be nice to know at whose behest. It's a reasonable question."

"You mean who actually signed the orders? God, how the hell would I know? What's that matter? I can't see why you're worked up about it."

"I don't suppose the name Cabot features?"

"*Cabot*? I've no idea. You really want to know?" Almost angry, Elton began pecking through the folder, snatching pages apart, stopping now and then to peer down.

"It's here I think. Yes, it does look like *Cabot*. Some kind of Under Secretary. Cabinet Office. I don't move in those circles. You've heard of him? You know who he is?"

"Enough to know he's dead."

Seeing Elton's puzzled stare, Alex made to get up. "In fact, well and truly dead when he signed those orders."

"*Dead*? What d'you mean, dead?"

"A train accident. Mr Cabot fell under a train."

"You mean he was pushed?"

"Interesting you should say that. I thought the same myself. No, apparently a completely regular accident. In another life I worked with him in a disinformation outfit. A unit called the TPSU. He was

16

our German language specialist. Don't get me started on Mr Cabot, but if you want to know why I managed to get myself cooped up in this place, how about a little bit of posthumous vengeance from a supercilious bastard who pushed people around like chess pieces, who didn't live to see the consequences of what he did. Look, Maurice, I'd better take myself off. I've a sermon to write for tomorrow's lot. Can't let the chaps down."

"Wait a minute. I want to get this straight. What had this man Cabot got against you? I'd like to know."

"It started with one of our agents captured. The Jerries started working him back to us. Cabot began playing along."

"Yes … I see." He was looking hard at Alex, "A bit cold blooded … but it happens. You have to take what chances you get. This agent? Someone you knew? I'm sorry ..."

"No, I didn't know the chap. And you don't see at all. Once Cabot saw it was working, he started feeding agents into the Jerry network."

"*Feeding*? I'm not following you. Or perhaps I am. But you can't mean ..."

"That's exactly what I do mean. He ended up dropping agents to certain capture - twenty or more. All for the advantage of Jerry thinking they owned them. One of those agents was me, by the way. The really perverse thing is, it damn well worked. Against all the odds, it came off perfectly. Textbook disinformation. Jerry never believed their own intelligence about the landings, even when it was staring them in the face. They swallowed every crafty lie Cabot fed through his army of fictitious doubles. It was incredible."

"But nobody in their right mind could have authorised that operation. It would be calculated murder. A war crime." He sat staring sightlessly down at the open folder waiting for Alex to say something.

"You're right. Obviously, you're right. Nobody could possibly authorise that. So nobody did. We were discouraged from asking who teed up all those drops. No, John Cabot worked alone. *Allegedly,* as the newspapers have it. I might have ended up feeling sorry for him if he hadn't been so damned superior - you're hellishly exposed when you're deniable. All the agents were shot, of course. When the game was up, Cabot must have guessed a train accident was on the cards."

"Who else knew about this? I mean of those out of the SOE loop?"

"Hard to say. Mrs Perry was one of the agents they captured. She might have guessed what was going on, but I'm not sure. We managed to get her out. More by luck than judgement - a rogue French agent fixed it – former Deuxième Bureau. Chap called Pascal Renault."

Elton allowed himself a faint smile, "*Pascal* - the right name anyway. You realise we had orders about Mrs Perry as well – you do realise that? Perhaps you didn't know ..."

"*About Justine*? Why the hell wasn't I told? What orders?"

"Calm down, Alex. I didn't even know who Mrs Perry was. Still don't for that matter. It was nothing out of the ordinary. In no circumstances were you to contact her." He shrugged, spreading his hands in a mock hopeless gesture. "That's how it was. A perfectly routine order, the usual guff about all best efforts to be employed and so forth, but no detail."

"And Cabot signed that as well, I suppose? Amazing what you can do when you're dead. Christ, how bloody obedient you all are."

"You're not seeing things straight Alex. You know we get orders like that every day. Standard instructions for dealing with doubles, absentees, rogue agents, you know ..."

"*Rogue agents*. Christ almighty! Do you know what they did to her when she ended up in France? D'you know? She was tortured. The bastard raped her. Is that in your damned file?"

Elton turned to look through the window, a slight flush of embarrassment on his face. "I'm sorry, Alex ... very sorry. No, it's not in the file, nothing like that."

"She killed him. Major Gliess. In Intelligence, the *Abwehr*. He ran a wireless station. We got her back home but that was the end of her service – her active service."

"I wasn't involved, Alex, I knew nothing about any of that. How could I? Nobody here knew anything about her, and that's the god's honest truth. Your file only arrived last week. But you're wrong about one thing, you know. She didn't resign. Mrs Perry is still listed as active. Section F. The French Desk."

"That's nonsense - of course she resigned. You know the rule – once captured, no going back. How long d'you think she would last? She's assassinated a Wehrmacht officer, for God's sake. There's a hell of a price on her head – mine too, I imagine. So I'll ask again: what orders?"

"Sorry, Alex, all this is way beyond my authority. Way over my head. It's a problem I could have done without."

"How d'you think I feel? Didn't I deserve to know?"

"Until this week I'd have been court-martialed for even mentioning it – and that's the truth."

"*This week*? You mean the landings?"

Elton laced the folder up, patting it like a dog, "That's what it says. *Until such time as the Allied invasion is underway*."

Alex stood up, turning to go, watching Elton fish in a drawer pulling at a box file bound with two rubber bands. "That's why she never replied to my letters ... of course she didn't."

"Here, you may as well take them. It's that or having them burned. They're all in there," Elton's face was still flushed with a kind of embarrassed pity. "God, Alex, what were we supposed to do? Letters meet the definition of *contact*. Obviously they do."

"And the stuff I asked the chaps in the Guardhouse to post?"

He pushed the box across the desk, avoiding Alex's eyes.

"They're all in there. You'd better take them."

# three

THE morning Alex finally left Torridon, Major Elton was not at breakfast. Rumour had it he had wangled a posting to London and would not be returning.

He would have had little to return to in any case. Station 402 Signals, having run its course, was to be abandoned to the sheep.

For Alex, release from the humiliation of his benign imprisonment had been ludicrously inconsequential: a letter in his mail box acknowledging he existed, listing his pay, and declaring him on indefinite leave.

It appeared to have been signed.

Possibly by Elton.

He had been a few weeks in London when the invitation arrived.

A card, deckle-edged in gilt, a little vulgar, addressed *as from* Boodles Club, announcing a Service of Thanksgiving to commemorate the life and work of Colonel Archer.

Remembering his distant TPSU days with Cabot, both of them under the old boy's command, it was difficult not to smile. Inexplicably placed in charge of a Disinformation Unit, it had been obvious to everyone that the ancient Colonel knew even less about disinformation than his batman.

*Thanksgiving*. Who on earth had Archer to thank for anything at all? A foolish old man left over from the wrong war. Coming so close on the landings, even the timing smacked of vanity - in the great calculus of war, Colonel Archer's tiny contribution to Normandy had been entirely accidental.

Perhaps he had bequeathed the funds himself, paying for people to praise his corpse - he was just about conceited enough.

All the same, Alex did not throw the card away, propping it up instead against the looking glass, alongside the forlorn pile of letters to Justine.

Something to glance at now and then.

As the days passed, he would take the card down to look at, reluctant to admit that he would accept, after all. It was not impossible, not entirely impossible. She had met Archer once. You could almost say she knew him.

Justine might be there.

Since getting back to London, his life had been no more than a search for Justine. It was all he did. Endless sallies against unyielding officialdom, each more futile than the last. He would return to the flat, hearing her voice as he stood at the locked door. Only for whatever sounds had deceived him to be absorbed into the still silence.

The dead days after Torridon were spent walking the burnt streets, consumed with the startling realisation that while he had been away people had somehow resolved themselves to couples. He would sit in restaurants alone, eating too quickly, the book propped open at the side of his plate unread, aware that people now came in pairs. Every woman of a certain build, perhaps reflected in some shop window, appeared like a reproachful ghost jolting his heart.

Imperceptibly, the brief time with Justine condensed into little more than a handful of vivid recollections suspended like crystals in the denser fluid of his memory. Terrified he might forget, he would

21

cling to tiny fragments of their past like scenes in some shadowy inconsequential film looping forever in his mind.

One scene above all others filled his sleepless nights. The Russell Hotel. Him turning to the sound of the opening door, affecting surprise. Justine slipping off her blouse, her eyes on his, laughing: *It's usual to take your clothes off. Here, shall I make a start? Time you were abed, young man.* Justine leaning over him, her breasts against his mouth. Justine's dark voice, suddenly gentle.

An awareness of what it might be to be happy.

In which case, *not impossible* seemed better than nothing.

*Notre Dame de France* the card said. Somewhere off Leicester Square. It seemed he knew the church, but could not remember why.

Catholic, for sure.

Another reason Justine might come.

*Not impossible.*

He would wander from room to room in the echoing empty flat, mumbling the phrase until it became a kind of maudlin emotional tic, setting his heart pounding. *The simple lack of her is more than others' presence* - where had he read that? He could not remember either. It seemed right enough.

After Torridon he had believed he was coming home. To discover that, without Justine, he had nowhere to come home to.


He was very late.

Picking a way through the maze of demolished buildings behind Leicester Square, he had got hopelessly lost, arriving to discover the service already underway.

Pushing the heavy felt-lined door, clammy ecclesiastical waves of candle heat met him, the church packed.

An ancient priest was intoning preliminary words in impenetrable Hungarian, *Archer* the only sound anyone recognised.

Alex stood alone at the back for the service, hypnotic Latin echoing from the fluted dome above.

Children's voices improbably floated out above dark ranks of sober suited men.

Justine was not among them.


It could not have been more than an hour.

They shambled out, blinking into pale spring sunshine, a field of rosebay willow herb swaying like purple corn in the gap across the road where the cinema had been. It gave the place a curious rural air. Hoards of scruffy urchins crawled among the stalks. *Fireweed* they called it, not unreasonably.

Alex found himself snaking single file down a flight of steps. Heaps of blackened brickwork all that was left of a town house.

Breaking away, he pushed up from the area yard fighting to reach the pavement, hoping for a taxi. He felt someone grab his arm, steering him towards an open door, alcohol and cigarette smoke surging out in hot waves.

"Didn't we meet at Tempsford once? I'm sure that's right. I do believe you were thinking of running away. Won't do, old chap."

Seeing Alex's expression, the tall figure at his side seemed offended.

"No, you don't know me from Adam, do you?"

Too late, Alex placed the face. The MO from the Interrogation Centre at Abbott Court. When had all that business been? Years ago. TPSU days, Archer in his pomp, Cabot, still alive and kicking. In those days you always needed a tame doctor for the sodium amytal.

He had not worn well. Older, he seemed unhappy in the open air, sallow cadaverous face the colour of war. There were dark purple smudges under his watery eyes. Untidy greyish hair had been pushed under an Air Force cap.

The uniform was blue, not completely clean, his rank lost beneath a long coat.

There was a kind of easy authority about the grip on Alex's arm.

"That's two of these things this month. Good enough show, I suppose. Apart from the Latin, can't abide Latin, reminds me of school. You worked for the old boy, didn't you? I suppose you knew he was Hungarian? Hence the priest they dug up to do the necessary. Do you go for all this Catholic stuff? You that way inclined?"

Watching the MO's incurious face, Alex looked away.

*No, but Justine was. The only woman I'll ever love. She was. That's why I came. It was not impossible - she might have been mad enough to come.*

He let the words echo in his mind, pondering escape, the MO leaning over him, mock-conspiratorial.

"Formidable chap, old Colonel Archer, so they say. Of course he was hardly *compos mentis* when I knew him, on account of his stroke. I'm right, aren't I? You did work for him?"

"I was in his unit, if you can call that work. I think formidable will do. You realise I wasn't his favourite son?"

"I guessed as much. You chaps were always at each other's throats those days. Some kind of cloak and dagger outfit, wasn't it? It's alright, you needn't agree."

"The TPSU. No, don't ask - I don't think we ever got told what the letters meant. We were a disinformation unit. But you're right, more dagger than cloak at the end. Mind you, quite effective, as things turned out."

He was talking too much. Alex stared round the roomful of strangers. "Look, I'd better not say any more. It's not over yet – isn't that what we're supposed to say?"

The MO tugged encouragingly on Alex's arm, "You don't have to, my boy. When you reach my age, the less you know, the better. It's a wicked world."

Shouldering a way through the crowd, he had found a chair for Alex, perching himself uncomfortably on a window sill.

"God, the noise in here. How d'you think we get a drink? I don't know why I bother. I keep saying this'll be the last. Then again, I suppose you can't help thinking it's your turn next." He barked out a laugh, "Not you, of course. You're just an infant," leaning forward to squeeze Alex's shoulder, "but I'm glad we've met up. Knew we would sooner or later. Something that's been exercising me. D'you mind if I ask you something?"

"Ask away. Sorry, I must have seemed a bit rude when you grabbed me up there. You took me by surprise."

The way to the door was blocked now, the room uncomfortably full.

"To tell you the truth, I didn't intend coming to this bit of the do. And then when you ... the thing is, I'm not very good with faces. Anyway, I felt I was barging in, rather. I'm amazed the old boy had so many friends. Frankly I'm surprised he had any."

"*Friends*? You mean the old Colonel? Here for the drink more like. Speaking of which ..." The MO launched himself forward, reaching over Alex's head, grabbing two glasses from a tray carried past by someone in a white coat.

"God, whisky. Somebody's stumping up. Mind you, Boodles isn't short of a bob or two. Can you see any water?"

Alex shook his head, watching the MO lean back on his perch, gingerly testing the weight of one shoulder against a leaded windowpane. This makeshift bar must once have been the housemaid's quarters.

"What was it you wanted to ask? Nothing complicated, I hope, You can't hear yourself think in here."

"Complicated? No, more by way of a *mea culpa*. Perhaps I should have looked you up at the time, but there you are. I was stuck in that hospital in St John's Wood doing guard duty over Colonel Archer. Keeping tabs on him in case he started talking, said the wrong thing, you know. That was after his stroke. The old boy expired on my watch, you realise. That's why I thought I ought to turn up to see him off."

He had stopped. Peering into his glass, working himself up to say something.

25

"Weird place, that hospital. Bars on the windows, that sort of thing. A bit demeaning for me, I can tell you - treated like a sort of hired nursemaid ... Still ... didn't you come out to see him?"

"Just the once. I wasn't to know it, but that was the last time I saw him. Now you mention it, I remember thinking the place a bit weird."

"More than a bit."

"I didn't say at the time. My lips were sealed. But Colonel Archer didn't have anything he could blab about. No secrets. He was a remarkably simple chap."

"Funny job to be in, if that's right."

"Oh, I don't know. Sometimes it serves to have an idiot in charge. Archer never really knew what he was mixed up in. That's why they couldn't risk him gossiping."

"Loose cannon, you mean?"

"Something like that. What's this you wanted to ask?"

"Nothing to do with Colonel Archer, God rest his soul. It's a bit awkward. It's about a colleague of yours. A Mr Cabot. I forget his other name. You remember him?"

"Of course I remember him. His name's John. John Cabot. We worked together for months. Right up until his accident. He was killed. Fell onto the tracks at Oxford station. It's funny, accidents shouldn't happen in wartime, don't you think? It seems excessive somehow. There's more than enough death to go round in a war without accidents."

Seeing the MO grimace, Alex tried to smile. "Sorry. Not in the best of taste. Silly idea anyway. Cabot's dead enough."

"That was the word - *accident*."

The MO barked the word out as if Alex had denied something. Pressing one hand into his eyes as if the smoke was annoying him. He leaned forward, staring intently into Alex's face, finally waving his glass at the crush of sweating men.

"You think that's all we're going to get?"

"Seems that way. Look, about John Cabot. If he was a friend of yours, I should say right off he was no friend of mine. In fact he was the bastard who managed to get me locked up."

"Come again."

"He had me posted to this sort of training centre. The place is closed down now. When I got there I found I couldn't get out. I ended up like Archer in your hospital, more or less for the same reason. I'd been very close to this chap Cabot. Knew things about him I couldn't be allowed to know – you follow me? It was decided I was best out of the way."

"Steady on, that's going it a bit, old man."

"You think I'm joking? I'm sure they considered the option of polishing me off, but it was decided all things considered I was better buried until D-Day. Deliverance Day, I call it. Of course Archer solved the problem by obligingly dying."

"What d'you mean, *decided*? Who thought that one up? And who the hell's *they* anyway?"

"John Cabot was one of that crowd at the London Controlling Section. That lot can do what they like ... no, it's alright, you don't need to agree. But you know it's true. We've got to win the war. One way or another. Best not to stand in the way."

"But this chap Cabot ... you think he really could?

"He had the authority alright. Something else he lied about. The risk was I might tell the world what he'd been up to in the TPSU."

"And what was that?"

Alex stared at him.

"Okay, shouldn't have asked." He looked mildly aggrieved, his face pink. "Fair enough ... right you are."

Relenting, Alex threw him a bone. "I can tell you this much. Cabot spent his time concocting stories, mostly for the enemy to swallow. He was extremely good at it, but not all that discriminating. He ended up lying to everybody. It was his speciality. I've thought since how best to describe him. The best I can come up with is *deformed*.

People like him are hellishly dangerous, not properly human. It's a hard thing to say, but I'm not sorry he's gone. The world's better off without people like that."

The MO looking unhappily round the room, vainly searching for rescue, lost for how best to put something.

"You appreciate, I didn't like it." Alex could barely hear him, "Being used that way. You know what I mean?"

"*Used*? This is Cabot we're talking about? I thought you said you didn't know him. You're right, he used people, rode roughshod if he got half a chance. A devious character. Do we have to talk about him?"

"I suppose not. Well … in a way, yes. I mean, I never knew him, nothing like that. What I'm saying is I resented being drawn into a put up job like that. Then finding he was behind it."

Unaccountably embarrassed, the MO was fumbling awkwardly in an inside pocket for his cigarette case, opening it for Alex, suddenly defiant. "Because that's what it was - a put up job."

Alex took a cigarette, waiting for the match, suddenly uneasy, "A put up job?"

"I mean whoever spun that yarn to me about the train accident must have known I'd pass it on. They knew I'm a talkative sort of chap. Can't be helped – that's the way I am. Makes you feel used, that sort of thing."

Alex laughed. "God, you're not going to tell me it wasn't an accident after all? I'm not surprised. You know what? He had it coming. So somebody pushed him after all?"

"You're not following me. I mean it was the people running the show … the people in London Controlling Section, don't you see? Your Mr Cabot is alive and well. I saw him myself a few days after Colonel Archer died. Had a few days leave after that bloody hospital. He came trotting down Baker Street, fine and dandy. Tipped his bowler at me. A bit shame-faced, now I think about it, but he didn't stop. That was when I realised I'd been taken for a mug. As I say, I was used. Didn't like it."

He seemed relieved to have got something off his chest, looking down, spinning the last of the drink in his glass.

"No, like I say, your Mr Cabot is no more dead than I am."

# four

THE room was quieter now, people drifting away into the afternoon. Alex sat on in silence, revising his world, painfully aware the task was beyond him, tangled threads breaking in his hands. He had never really believed in Cabot's accident, certain that someone had pushed him, content to leave it at that.

It hardly mattered: the man was gone. Dead was dead.

But dead was not dead. *Dead* was very much alive.

And remembering the pile of letters on his mantelpiece, Alex flushed with sudden panic. *Gullible* - hadn't Cabot once called him that? It had seemed almost a compliment at the time, a kind of exoneration, purchasing no more than a modest sense of shame, excusing him from the worst. From the sordid truth of the life they lived.

Thoughts of Justine flooded into his mind, thoughts he dared not properly pursue. What had he said in all those intercepted letters? Dozens of them. All those futile cries were not simply witness to Justine's loss. With Cabot alive, each word had risked her death. What had he written? All those, incautious, stupid, poisoned words: *what the hell had he written?* The question seemed barely worth the asking. Too much, he was sure of it. Reaching out to Justine could well have been the surest way of ensuring she would never be found.

At the far end of the room a group of men wearing the Boodles tie had crowded round a piano, vainly trying to remember the words of some music hall song. The MO looked nostalgically across, lips mumbling half remembered words. Seeing Alex's face he shook his head apologetically.

"Sorry, it's been more of a shock than I thought, I can see that. And there was me thinking it wasn't all that important."

He fixed Alex's face, a show of fake contrition, "Look here, I'd have told you if I'd known where you were. That was the trouble. Where were you?"

"Scotland."

"Rather you than me. Too bloody cold."

"That was not the only reason to avoid the place, believe me."

Alex pulled back his sleeve, throwing a ritual glance at his watch, "I'd better be off. Some things I need to look through. God … all that time. I thought he was dead. Sure of it."

The MO looked away, rolling the glass between his hands.

Alex hoisted himself on tiptoes, nodding towards the open door. "It's alright, you know. Nobody's fault. Well, mine, I suppose. It's not even that I was taken in – I took myself in. I was so damned sure the man was dead."

He flinched as the MO lunged past his head, clutching the sleeve of a reluctant waiter, bringing him up short, liberating two more drinks, pressing one into his hand.

Alex took it, "Alright, just this one. Then I do need to get back. Things to think about. Homework. *Revision* we used to call it. Plenty of that now, given your so-called accident."

The MO looked pained. "It wasn't *so-called* when I passed that message on. You believe what you're told, don't you? Well, I do. Okay, it wasn't true, I know that now, but how the devil are you supposed to arm yourself against bare-faced lies?"

He looked tired: an old man blinking into a whisky glass.

31

Alex took pity on him. "Oh, that's easy. *Assume everybody is lying.* Of course, it ruins your social life, but it gets you by. John Cabot taught me that rule – he just forgot to explain it applied to him. To tell you the truth – that's a joke, by the way – I'd convinced myself he'd been pushed. People like Cabot don't just die and accidents were easy to arrange in those days. It was best to look the other way."

He perched his glass, still full, on the windowsill next to the MO's. "Now I'm off. I won't thank you for the news, but I'll try to accommodate to it. Mind you, should I believe it? Bearing in mind Mr Cabot's famous rule."

The MO managed a nervous laugh, "Now you're teasing me. It's true alright. I saw him as close as you are now, scout's honour." He raised himself up on his perch, scanning the emptying room. "It crossed my mind he might have come to this do. Archer was his boss, after all."

"He wouldn't have put it that way. But that's a story for another time."

Alex followed the MO's gaze through the blue haze of smoke. The crowd had thinned a little, those left behind determined to see the afternoon out, little knots of men standing too close, capping each other's jokes with sudden bursts of barking laughter. Resolutely masculine, all of it. If women had played any part in Archer's life it had been a secret he took with him. Stupid to imagine Justine walking into an affair like this - she had more sense.

The MO had jumped down, standing almost too close, earnestly searching Alex's face.

"You were miles away there, old chap. I could see it in your eyes. I know exactly what you're thinking. No women. That's what you were thinking, isn't it? I'm the same. I hate these men-only things."

"I suppose so. Actually, it was just possible someone might have been …"

"… At that service? No, there's never women … well, the odd widow, but not otherwise. You'd be out of luck there. None at this

32

one, anyway, not so much *rara avis* as *avis invisibilia*. God, all that Latin must have got to me." Starting a choking laugh, he checked himself, his head rearing back, as if seeing Alex for the first time.

"Damned silly rule, this not exchanging names. Who dreams them up? Y'know your name's just come to me. I remember now." He lowered his voice to a theatrical whisper, "You're Captain Vere, aren't you? It's just clicked. Been plaguing me ever since I saw you outside the church. You're the chap came out to the hospital to see the old Colonel ... Colonel Archer ..."

"Better late than never for introductions, I'm Alex Vere ... I doubt I'll be shot for telling you ..."

The MO ignored his outstretched hand, raising his own, palm forward as if stopping traffic.

"No, wait ... it was you Archer was going on about in that hospital. Alex Vere, that's the name. You and some missing woman. He went on about it for days on end. *Gone missing*, he kept saying. Y'know what he did then?" Alex shook his head, suddenly alert, reaching out to rescue his glass, conscious of the rising thud of his heart. "I'll tell you what. He ordered the nurses to phone the Russell Hotel, of all places. Said he knew she was there. Really agitated."

"Oh, that old story." Hearing the disappointment in Alex's voice, the MO looked puzzled. "I thought for a minute it was something else. That's an ancient story. When Colonel Archer was in charge of the TPSU, an agent went AWOL. He tracked her down to the Russell Hotel. The old boy was incredibly pleased with himself - fancied himself as Hercule Poirot. He must have been thinking about that."

"You may be right. All the same, he talked me into traipsing across the town with a letter."

"What? To the Russell Hotel? But that business was years ago ..."

"I could have been in trouble for leaving my patient, but he was so worked up it seemed best to humour him. I sorted out a nurse to cover for me very early one morning. The Colonel was always asleep then. To tell you the honest truth, we made sure he was asleep."

"But there would be nobody there. There couldn't be. At the hotel, I mean ..."

The sudden urgency in Alex's voice brought an odd cautious look to the MO's face, realising he was trespassing on foreign soil.

"There was actually. Name of Perry - I knew the name would come to me. Bloody funny place to hide, I must say, but Archer had been absolutely right. There she was, large as life. It was hellishly early and the woman on the desk made me wait, but eventually she came down."

"Who came down? You mean Justine Perry? You actually met her?"

"Had breakfast together. All very civilised, very pleasant. I remember she said she'd stayed there when she was a kid. I suppose that was why she'd picked the place."

Seeing the whisky in his glass trembling, Alex gripped it hard in two hands, pressing it into his chest.

"And this letter of Archer's?"

"*Letter*? Oh, yes - what about it? I gave it to her and she read it right there in front of me. Stuffed it in her bag. Nothing else."

"Look, exactly when was all this? No ... sorry ... I shouldn't press you. But it means the hell of a lot to me. D'you remember when exactly?"

"When Archer sent me off on this errand, you mean? You could work it out for yourself. Around the time you came out to see him at the hospital. It would be a few days before, I think. Is it important? I wouldn't make too much of that letter if I were you. He was very muddled at the end ... dying, you know. Strokes take people like that. They get an idea into their head and ruminate on it endlessly. Probably decided to send her something he'd cut out of a newspaper – that happens. You say he'd traced somebody to that hotel before, well, there you are. He couldn't shake it out of his head. Look, that waiter's avoiding us. If we want a drink I think we'll have to find somewhere else."

"No, thanks all the same. I'm off. All this has been a bit of a shock. I should have explained, I've been looking for Justine Perry for a long time. We were very close."

The MO clambered back onto his windowsill, steadying himself against Alex's shoulder.

"I think I'll stay on a bit. Nothing else to do. This Perry name. I've gone and stirred things up, haven't I? I'm always doing it. Comes from living on my own. You get out of the way of talking to people, and then when you do ... seems I'm saying sorry again ... talking out of turn."

He summoned up an expression of ritual concern, not entirely convincing. "So you never found her?"

"No. Hearing you just then, I felt cheated somehow. You'd managed to meet her, pat like that, when I'd drawn a blank. I went to the Russell myself, but she wasn't there. She'd gone."

The MO reached out, resting his hand on Alex's arm, "Actually, I did see her again. Steady on, old chap, don't jump on me. Only in a manner of speaking."

"What the hell's that mean? Sorry ... sorry. *In a manner of speaking*? What's that mean?"

"I've seen a painting of her. If you give me a sec I'll remember where I saw it. I'm certain it's her. Not somebody you forget, is she?" He started tapping his cheek, mumbling to himself, "Where was it? Where was it?"

"*A painting*? Of Justine? No, you must be wrong."

"I'm right, I tell you. Look, d'you want to know or don't you?" Screwing his face into a frown, "I'm trying to think. It was long time ago. Where the hell was it?"

"I wasn't doubting you. I just can't understand. A *painting*? And you're sure it's her?"

"Got it! *Carters*, that's the place. New Bond Street. I used to pass it every day. And yes it's her. The woman I had breakfast with."

"Justine Perry?"

35

"If you say that's her name. I'd stake my life on it."

"A portrait?"

"I suppose you could say a portrait. A bit modern for my taste, but it's her alright. All on its own in the window, I remember. No price ticket on it. That means too pricey for the hoi polloi, doesn't it? Now you're going to ask who painted it. The artist and all that. Not a clue, old boy. Pictures aren't my cup of tea. But I remember the title. I stood looking at it because the title seemed a bit obvious. She'd been got up in a straw hat, you see."

"And the title?"

"*Girl in a Straw Hat*. Well, it was in French actually, but you're not getting me practising the accent on a professional. Easy enough, though, even for me. A girl in a straw hat - that's what it said. Carters – you know where they are? Why don't you go and ask?"

# five

*D* UNDEE. A weird little place clinging to the banks of the river Tay, its only easy access the flimsy lattice of an iron bridge. The second bridge, to be precise: the rusty stumps of the last effort still visible.

Alex went into the corridor to watch the train launch itself improbably above the river, riveted columns of the bridge grinding past. Trails of creamy spume swirled in with the tide, seals fighting for space on shrinking sandbanks.

The sun had gone, leaving a vast luminous vapour the colour of blood hanging over the city.

The station was a grubby warren of gas-lit passageways leading up to air smelling of the sea. Twin slate towers to his left reared over the town like some strange Assyrian monument, a white arc of letters plastered to its side: *The Queen's Hotel.*

Her letter was waiting for him at the desk:

*Dear Captain Vere,*

*Of course, I remember you. It seems a long time ago. Carters said you might write, so you have not really taken me by surprise.*

*Yes, I can tell you something about that painting. We can meet at almost any time – my hours are my own, although I have things to do tomorrow morning. The big store opposite the City Churches has a tea room. I will try to be there at noon. Bear with me if I am a little late.*

*Lucile Beyrou*

The following morning he walked to Draffen's Store, stationing himself in sight of the double doors to watch her come. He would wait a little then follow her inside. Or *them*. Surely that was the word? Why else would she say she had things to do? He had feasted on that thought through a troubled night, waking to the certainty of it.

She would be bringing Justine with her.

He stood for half an hour in a chill wind, hardly knowing what he would say, smiling to think she would ease the way, Justine was like that. Perhaps she would mock him just a little. He could hear her now, laughing at his earnest wind-pinched face: hear her dark voice – after how many lost hours – teasing him for standing in the cold.

The church clock at his back forced him into the heat of the shop, feeling foolish, taking the stairs two at a time, bursting breathless into the panelled tea room on the floor above.

The place seemed empty, no sound but the echo of Justine's remembered voice.

Then he saw. Not empty. Lucille Beyrou sat alone at the far end, by a window, a paper parcel tied with string at her feet. She must have been here long before he arrived, watching him in the street.

She stood as he reached the table, letting him shake her hand.

"Captain Vere. I was worried I wouldn't recognise you. Thank goodness you've not changed."

Her voice was oddly familiar, hesitant, like her letter. She seemed nervous, darting eyes taking in his uniform.

"I'm afraid it's just tea. I've ordered."

"Tea is welcome. I've been standing in the cold. You must have seen me. I got here early. Hoping to beat you to it."

"I've been thinking ..." pausing to let a tram grind past outside, "trying to remember where it was. Somewhere in Bedford Square, is that right? That time we met? I remember there were stairs."

She was fussing with the lid of a metal teapot, pushing a tiny milk jug towards him.

"I didn't ask for sugar ... forgot the coupons ..." She stopped, idly turning the tiny spoon round and round, watching the spinning circle in her cup.

Thinner than when she had climbed those stairs at the TPSU, she looked vaguely unwell, her forehead misted with sweat although the room was cool. But the smile when it finally touched him was friendly, a tiny apologetic moue, confirming what he had known since he saw she was alone: she bore news he would not want to hear.

"I didn't mean to spy. You looked cold standing in the wind like that. Dundee's never really warm, you know." She stopped again, looking down at her cup, her voice suddenly tense: "I would have come down, but I saw it wasn't me you were looking for."

She was rubbing at a tiny fleck of something red on the heel of her thumb.

"She's not here. I thought you would know. Did you think she might be? I'm sorry if I led you to think that."

The place was filling up, a chatter of lunch-time voices, women mostly, wrapping itself round the awkward silence.

"No, no, you didn't lead me to think anything. I was deceiving myself. I deceive myself a lot - it's become a habit lately. Keeps my spirits up. Looking for someone is such a dispiriting business. After a while ... I mean ... you have days when you know you'll never find her. You won't know what it's like. I wouldn't wish it on anybody. Sometimes you think you're going a little mad. I find myself recognising complete strangers, it's humiliating ..."

She paced out a beat, measuring the seconds, staring quietly at his face, perhaps hoping to read something there.

"Oh, I know all about that. A long time ago, but I know exactly what you mean. What I meant was you coming all this way on a false prospectus, thinking she might be here. I feel responsible."

She finished her tea, summoning up a faint smile. "Hope's miserable stuff isn't it? I quite wore myself out with it once. A long time ago. This damned war."

Alex had the impression she had forgotten he was there. She sat frowning at the mass of faces around them, as if wondering how they had appeared. She seemed to be talking to herself.

"There was somebody on the wireless the other day. He said it was our duty to hope for the best. I'm not sure about that." She looked up, gathering her thoughts, again the brief flash of a smile, "Well ... here you are anyway. To talk about a painting ..."

"Sheer chance really. Funny how things are often like that. D'you remember talking about Justine Perry that day you came to see me at Bedford Square? And please don't worry about my coming all this way. It means a lot to me just to meet somebody who knew Justine. It was such an extraordinary thing – I met somebody who said you'd painted a portrait of her. That's how I tracked you down. I winkled your address out of the people at that gallery. They weren't all that keen, but I told them about Justine and they relented."

She smiled, hearing the name pronounced in the French manner, shaking her head, remembering something.

"I seem doomed to disappoint you, Captain Vere. You do realise the painting's not here. So if you were hoping ... didn't Carters tell you?"

"That the painting had not been intended for sale but somebody bought it all the same. Yes, they told me that. They said you weren't at all happy."

40

"They were right about that! But is that all they said? They didn't tell you who bought the painting? Surely …"

"No, they didn't tell me that. They didn't tell me anything. The chap could see I was there to get your address: I was worried he would throw me out. I got it in the end."

"But didn't you say who you were? Didn't they want to know?"

Alex frowned, "We tend not to volunteer names. It's something that comes with the job, I'm afraid. Regulations. And I was in uniform. That always seems to induce deference, God knows why."

"Then you don't know who bought it?"

Alex shook his head, reaching for his cigarette case, puzzled by the sudden intensity in her voice.

"It was you! Carters wrote to me, saying it had been bought by someone called Alex Vere. A cash sale. And yes, you're right. I was irritated they'd let it go but I could see why you might have wanted it."

"This is the first I've heard of it - it's nonsense. Somebody must have used my name. The first I knew about this painting was a couple of weeks ago. Look, are you sure it wasn't Justine herself? Perhaps she got somebody to do the deal?"

"No, it wasn't that. It couldn't have been. The people at Carters remembered the man. Then when they started to do the paperwork it turned out the address was somewhere bombed out years ago." Her smile was suddenly warm, "Please don't look so worried – I knew at once it wasn't you. A tubby chap, they said," glancing at his uniform, "and nobody would call you tubby, would they? Short sighted with big pebble lens glasses. Oxford accent. Well turned out, sporting a rolled umbrella. Impressively up to speed on modern painting. Carters assumed he was from a gallery. Actually impersonation happens quite a bit in the art world. Disreputable people looking for ways of getting a better price. It sounds like a mystery, but …"

Seeing something in his face her voice petered out.

For a few seconds, before reality imposed itself, it had seemed to Alex that he must embrace two contradictory truths: Cabot laid to rest in some Oxford churchyard, long dead; Cabot very much alive, haunting Bond Street galleries.

She was waiting for him to speak, both acutely aware of the silence between them.

He felt suddenly lightheaded, thoughts of Justine's vulnerability engulfing him.

"I'm sorry, what were you saying? Getting a better price … yes. I was thinking about something else. This tubby chap. Did he give a name?"

"But I told you. Your name."

She reached out, briefly resting her hand on his, pressing it against the tablecloth. "I know it had nothing to do with you."

"I'm not so sure about that. It must have been somebody who knew me, to use my name. In fact, he knew me very well indeed."

"He did? I don't understand." Her face had closed on him, suddenly wary.

"He's from my world, not yours. My former world, I should say. He worked with me in that unit in Bedford Square … the place you visited."

"But why my painting?"

"It's the sort of weird thing he did for a living, if you can call it that. He was given to telling lies. In fact I thought he was dead, but that turned out to be yet another lie."

As she started to say something, Alex turned his head away, mumbling to himself, "Cabot had a reason for everything ... he must have had a reason. No, not *had* … I mean *has*. That's what frightens me. Sorry … just give me a minute, I have to think. Why was he interested in that painting? He must have had a reason. *Why?*"

Across the road people huddled at the tram-stop were unfurling umbrellas. His silence became infectious, women at the next table glancing nervously across.

"I didn't sign things *Beyrou* – if that's relevant." She was struggling for his attention. "That was the only time. What I mean is, he can't have wanted it for my name." She was blushing, "People did, you know, when I used my own name. That's the only painting I've ever signed Beyrou. That's why Carters got mixed up."

It was some time before Alex spoke, his face clearing. He had barely been listening.

"No, it wasn't the signature. He bought it because of Justine. He will know she had been here, because you painted it – that's why he was interested. Look, can you tell me what brought her to Dundee. Can you do that?"

She shifted to the edge of her chair, reaching down to the parcel at her feet.

"I went to get some sketches this morning. I'd lent them to somebody. They're of Justine. Do you have time to come to the College? It's coming on to rain, but if we run, it's not far. I can tell you what I know. Then you can tell me all about Paris. I never imagined I'd miss France so much. I'm greedy for news."

"*Paris?* What about Paris?"

But she was already standing at the little counter by the door, shaking coins out of her purse to settle the bill.

The walk to Bell Street took them through the Houff graveyard. The rain stopped as they pushed through the iron gates. She walked ahead, pausing to wait for him, resting her parcel on a gravestone set back a little from the gravel path - a single chiselled skull over crossed bones, cavernous eyes widened by centuries of rain staring past the brown paper to the sky.

"I wanted to show you this. It looks best when the weather's grey. I used to come here when I first arrived. That's after your people got me out of France."

"Not really my people. Of course, I knew they'd got you out, because Justine was involved. It was her mission, not mine."

She perched one shoe on the edge of the stone. "Somehow it got into my first Dundee painting. I'd only been here a few weeks ... I

43

wasn't in the best of shape. Here, look ..." tugging his sleeve, pulling him to the foot of the grave, "they were monks. Franciscans. Crossed arms was their sign: did you know that? I imagine it means peace, fellowship, love ... something like that."

She waited until Alex looked down at the huge triangular slab of stone.

"Only they're bones, not arms. So it's all a sick kind of joke about death."

She had already set off towards the other gate, calling back to him.

"This is the way out. Dundee is full of graveyards. The place is made of bodies: I hate it."

# six

HER studio was much larger than he expected. And colder, the smell of turpentine barely defeating the pervading damp. It must have been a classroom once, little used, tucked away on the fourth floor: bare wooden boards stained with paint, a white china sink in one corner. Unframed canvasses were stacked three deep round the walls.

The windows looked across to a cliff of red stone tenements on the other side of the road.

She dragged out two wooden chairs, waving him into one, standing for a moment alongside him. She seemed uncomfortable, scanning the room, as if seeing the place through his eyes and finding it wanting.

A huge cranked easel draped in a piece of blue cloth stood in the centre of the room next to a pine table piled with crushed tubes of paint. He stared at the covering cloth thinking whatever was created in this chill place must surely have been hard won.

"I'm used to that look, Captain Vere."

She slumped down beside him, her smile surprisingly warm.

"Immune, you might say. I'm afraid I can't satisfy your curiosity. I'm superstitious about showing work in progress." Laughing, she seemed suddenly pretty, "Anyway, it's one of a series – I would have to make you see them all." The smile evaporated.

45

"But that's not why we're here, is it?"

"No, I wasn't thinking that. I just realised this is the second time I've been in your studio. Did you know?" She frowned at him, puzzled. "The first time was with Justine. In France. She was not in a good state. We only got away by the skin of our teeth. We'd just about managed to make the safe house. We called it that. It looks as if we were in your studio - this room is set out just the same way. I remember it was a stone building set apart from a big house. Perhaps Justine told you ... There was a portrait on an easel."

"Oh, you mean Albert Bradley's house? Yes, she told me a bit about that."

"The place is locked up."

"Not all the time. Albert still works there. He's far too famous for anything like a war to trouble him. He spends a lot of time in Paris now - it's that or starving I imagine. But you'll know about all that. I lived in that house for most of my professional life. No home of my own, that's what Mother used to say. But it wasn't my studio you were in, it was his - you know, Bradley's. You do know he had Germans billeted on him after I left? I imagine that was the end of it as a safe house."

"On the contrary – that's exactly what made the place uniquely safe. German troops were cover, you see. Horribly dangerous, of course, but I'd say Bradley's house became the most significant refuge in the South West."

"I never knew. And there was me thinking of him all alone. Apart from trips to Paris, of course. You must have come across him there."

"Paris? Why Paris?"

"Wasn't that where you were stationed?" She was blushing, a faint pink alteration to the pale of her cheeks. "God, she said I wasn't supposed to know. There, I confess - Justine told me."

"Justine told you I was in Paris? Where did she get that idea? I haven't been in Paris since I was a boy. Look, perhaps you'd better start at the beginning."

"You mean when she came to Dundee? It was over a year ago. March, I think. There's never a proper spring here, that's the first thing everybody learns. I remember it was so cold I was working in gloves. It was very late. I paint a lot at night. A porter came up to the studio, banging on the door. I thought he'd come to complain about seeing the lights, but it wasn't that. He said there was a woman asking for me downstairs. That was a time they left the main doors open, in case of a raid."

"And it was Justine?" Alex realised his heart was drumming. "Is that what you're saying?"

"Remember we'd only met once, I didn't recognise her. There was just this figure standing in the hall looking up the stairs. It was dark with the blackout and being pregnant changes the line of the body, the posture. Then when she spoke, I remembered her voice ..."

"Pregnant."

"She said she'd been on a train all day. Diverted somewhere. It's a hellish journey at the best of times. She was very tired ... completely lost. This place was all she could think of. She was asking about somewhere to stay. It was the middle of the night ..."

"What are you saying? You're saying she's pregnant? You mean Justine?"

"It was over a year ago."

"I didn't know."

He stretched one hand out towards her as if pushing her words away.

"I didn't know. She said nothing. No ... stop a minute ... I want to think."

She let him sit, silently searching his face, finally murmuring, "I'm sorry, that was very clumsy. You mean she hadn't ... yes, I can see why she wouldn't ..."

Alex went to the window, staring blindly into the street, trying to catch a little air. "But why would she come here? *Why*? I don't understand."

He turned to face her. "When was all this? When exactly?"

"I told you, March. I'm not sure of the date. But I can tell you why she came. She was looking for you. There had been a rumour you were in Scotland. She'd been here before, it was all she could think of. I don't think she was thinking very clearly. She seemed desperate, demented almost. I can only tell you what she said. She said you'd vanished."

She stopped, searching his face for some kind of reassurance. "And now here you are saying exactly the same thing - that's she's vanished."


Outside, the rain had started again, slanting in gusting wind. Alex stood at the window watching a couple of students run for shelter. The girl let the boy pull her into a doorway. They stood close, their heads touching.

When Elton had handed him that pile of letters it had seemed like the last move in a grubby game that had ended with Cabot dead on Oxford station. An end to something. He could take up a kind of life, re-set things, find what remained of a war to fight. Find Justine. Whatever the reasons for keeping them apart, they were surely spent. It only remained to find her, somehow to untangle the threads.

With Cabot dead, they could start again.

Except Cabot was not dead. Not dead at all.

The sound of pattering rain against the windowpanes filled the silence inside the studio. Lucile Beyrou sat immobile next to her secret canvas, her hands resting calmly in her lap. There was a steady pulse to a blue vein in her neck. How many lonely hours must she have spent in this desolate place?

She was waiting for him to say something.

"The last time I saw her ..." He could think of no other place to start. "We were in my flat in London. We'd been staying there after France. Waiting. I spend a lot of my life waiting. I had to go to a meeting that morning. When I got back, Justine had gone. She'd taken her things, not that there was very much, a suitcase, I think. I have not seen her since. That's how I lost her."

"*Lost?*"

"I got back from the meeting. I was to be posted to Scotland the next day. She'd gone. There was no note. Nothing."

"But that's not quite lost, is it?" The expression in the clear eyes meeting his own was suddenly less certain. "Perhaps you going away seemed the wrong time to tell you about the baby. She would have thought that."

"She left her ring on the table."

"Her ring? Then you're married. Justine didn't tell me. I didn't know that."

"No, we're not married. I was just trying to remember what happened that day. That seems very vivid to me. It was as if everything that day had some special meaning. I remember she'd been arranging flowers in a vase. Tulips. She started crying ... left the flowers scattered over the table. That was where I found the ring."

"But not a wedding ring?"

"No, it was something she'd always worn. Somebody she'd known a long time ago. A man. I'd better not start explaining, I'd only make a hash of it. You could the guess the story anyway. I've spent a year thinking about that ring. It sounds stupid, but you can't help trying to make sense of things. You say she thought I might be here? Why?"

"All I know is she said she was looking for you. The night she came to the College, it must have been two o'clock. Too late for hotels. I took her home with me, at first, just for somewhere for her to stay while she found her feet, but we fell into the way of it. I remember we sat up talking most of that night. I ended up talking about Oscar. She is the only person I've told that story to."

"Oscar?"

She sprang up, walking over to the other side of the room, taking a tiny framed photograph down from a shelf, holding it out to him.

49

"Would you like to see? He's on the left. Sorry, it's not much of a snap ..." She seemed reluctant to let go, "I wasn't to know this was all I'd have of him." Staring down at him her expression seemed hollowed out, bleak.

"We have that much in common. We've both lost somebody. Irrevocably, in my case. He's dead."

Alex bent his head over the tiny frame, a sepia echo of a time long ago when photographs were posed. A line of children sitting awkwardly on a lawn, the shadow of a white parasol suggesting a sun too high for England. In the distance, geraniums trailed from the windows of a stone house. The bulky shadow of whoever was holding the camera reached out towards the stiff line of seated figures.

"I recognise the place. Our safe house."

"That was before the war. When we were children we used to call it the Pink House."

A tall boy holding a tennis racquet stood a little apart from the others, his shoulders lost against the edge of the silver frame: aristocratic face, crinkly close-cropped hair. He looked bored. Her finger hovered over the photograph, not quite touching it.

"That's Oscar. You can see I'm looking at him."

"You were very young, just a little girl."

Glancing up at the pale face brooding over him Alex wondered where he was being led.

"And the prudent one who'd remembered her sun hat. Was she always so solemn?"

"That's my sister. You're right about the prudent bit. She was always playing mother." She eased the frame from his hands. "Laura and I haven't spoken for years. She never forgave me for staying behind in France when war broke out. It was as if I'd let her down, betrayed her. I suppose she's right. I only thought about my work then. Still do, if the truth's to be told."

She put the frame back on the shelf, straightening it, standing with her back to him. He could barely hear her. "So I never told her about Oscar. She would have thought I was trading misery. She knows nothing about him. Nobody knows ... except Justine ..." There was something burnt-out about her voice. "... And you now. You understand?"

As she turned he felt her look cool on his face. "Oscar was the only man I've ever loved. He was half of me, really ..." She stopped. "Now I'm embarrassing you."

"Of course you're not. I understand. *Irrevocable* is a hard word. I won't accept it."

"I told you because of Justine, don't you see? I tried to paint a kind of explanation. Something for her. It wasn't enough."

"I want to ask about the painting. The man who bought it ..."

"Oh, him - he doesn't matter. What mattered was painting her." She shrugged, the tiny gesture conceding something, "Well, alright, I admit I was irritated Carters let him buy it. I wanted Justine to have it. But it doesn't matter."

"I think it does matter. It matters a great deal."

## seven

"DID Justine tell you about what happened on her last mission? When she was dropped at Saint Aunix? Did she tell you why she resigned her commission?"

"She didn't talk about missions. She said she had been captured. She started to tell me what they did, but I got too upset. You have to understand I'm a feeble soul. All I do is paint. She could see I'm not very strong. She was strong enough for both of us. I suppose that was why she did that job. It all seems unimaginable to me."

"When an agent is captured strength doesn't come into it. Strong, weak - it makes no difference. All you know when you're captured is that the outcome is inevitable, that's why suicide's an option. I've spent my life these past few months teaching agents to accept the logic of suicide. Not Justine, though. She wouldn't."

"You mean because of her religion? Not *wouldn't*, surely? You mean *couldn't*?"

"That's how she sees it. I never understood. I realise now that's why they tortured her. There was no other reason. She had no information of value, nothing they didn't already know. She had to be diminished somehow. They made her believe she'd betrayed us."

She let the tiny silence spin out between them, both aware of unsayable words.

"She would flinch sometimes if you touched her hand. She told me everything about that man." Her voice was very calm. "Everything. How can people like that exist?"

"He didn't do that. People like Major Gliess don't like the sight of blood. People like him don't torture people, nothing so vulgar. He wanted something more obvious. You have to understand, not many field agents were women in those days. When Justine started, women were an exception. For Major Gliess, the injury was incidental."

Seeing his face she stretched out her hand, placing it on his.

"He raped her. Justine told me."

Feeling Alex ease his hand away, she held on, "No, let me explain. It was the only time I saw her cry. Telling me about that dreadful man. She knew what you would imagine. She said it meant nothing set against finding you."

"How can it mean nothing? You say she was pregnant."

"I didn't understand at first. It drove me mad. She seemed so … I'm not sure of the word … so *accepting*. I thought, if she won't take revenge, I'll damn well take it for her. That's why I wanted to paint her. I can't do much for this miserable world but I've got my work. God almighty – are you surprised I wanted to paint her … after hearing what she had to say?"

She sat restlessly running her thumb against the material of her dress, staring at the covered easel, letting tears well into her eyes.

"She told me about herself. Perhaps even things you don't know. We used to talk a lot about love. Like two schoolgirls. About you, of course, but I realise now I did most of the talking. She let me talk about my Oscar and I loved her for that. It was a sort of consolation. That's how we settled she would stay until the baby."

Seeing the pain in his face she looked away.

Alex leaned forward taking her arm, his voice suddenly urgent. "The baby. You mean the baby's here?"

"No, no, I'm getting things out of order. Justine was only here for a few weeks. I finished her painting quite quickly. Sent it off with some other stuff to Carters for framing. They seemed to take an awfully long time sending it back. Eventually, I discovered there had been a mix-up and they'd sold it. I was furious. It was about that time these two men came to the College. They said something to do with Justine's Identity Card. They looked like a couple of bank clerks. Very polite. I let the three of them have this studio. They spent most of the morning talking. That evening I remember Justine was in this strange mood. She made me swear a sacred oath I wouldn't breathe a living word to a soul. Then she said she knew you were in Paris. Alive and well and safe in Paris."

"Paris! But that's mad! How could I be in Paris? It's complete nonsense. You said yourself she'd heard I was in Scotland. And I was. When did all this happen? Are you sure that's what she said?"

She ignored him, painful eyes far away, struggling to recover something.

"I thought she should have been happy finding out where you were. Well, *relieved*, at least. But she wasn't. She seemed almost sullen. That night over dinner she blurted out she expected she'd leave soon. Just like that. It was such a funny way of putting it – as if she had nothing to do with it."

"You mean leave because of these men?"

"I'm not sure what I mean. I don't think so. She seemed angry about something."

She fetched the brown paper parcel from the table, pressing it into his hand. "It was the night I did these sketches. Here, take them, they're yours. No, not now. Open it when you find her. You'll see the way she looked - like some kind of avenging fury."

"When was this exactly? When these men came? Please - it's important: do you know the date?"

"I would have to look. April or May, I suppose. Yes, I think it was May, because the same men came back asking to see her urgently. Everything changed after that. That afternoon she said she was

54

leaving. It was all terribly abrupt. Strange how war makes things like that seem normal."

"Leaving where to?"

"It seemed mad but I remember asking her whether she was going to Paris. She didn't completely deny it. All I know is she seemed completely furious."

"Furious at leaving?"

"It seemed more than that. She left the next day. In a big car. It looked official. I remember I felt very let down - angry, I suppose. It's shameful, but all I remember thinking was that I'd not get that portrait back. I'm ashamed of myself. But I'd had them put the title on the frame. I had so much wanted her to see it. Trying to be clever, I suppose."

"What title?"

"*Fille au Chapeau de Paille*. After that painting by Bradley. The one he painted for his dead lover."

"I'm not sure I understand."

"You will when you see the painting. Remember I was thinking about Albert and about the baby. It's why I painted it. Just so you know."


On the other side of the road a little weak sunlight had coloured the buildings red. She stood up and went to the window, turning to look about the room, putting an end to something.

"I'm glad the rain's stopped. I was bothered you'd have to walk in the rain."

She seemed puzzled he made no effort to move. "I feel guilty letting you come all this way. It was selfish. The truth is I wanted to talk about her. And all I've done is talk about myself. Apart from telling you something you probably didn't want to know, I've been no help at all."

"Can you give me a few more minutes?"

She came back to him, sitting down, leaning towards him. "Of course, of course, stay as long as you like. But honestly I've told you all I know."

"I wanted to tell you about the man who bought your picture."

"Oh, that. What about him?"

"When I was posted to Scotland I found myself in a kind of benign captivity. The man responsible was called John Cabot. He was the man who bought your painting."

"How strange. So you do know him, after all?"

"I knew him very well indeed. In fact I worked with him. Secret work. We were involved in D-Day planning. After that, he saw to it I was kept out of harm's way for over a year."

"Why on earth?"

"I'd ended up knowing too much for my own good. I'd stumbled onto something by accident. Actually, I should count myself lucky. Cabot's usual method was much more radical."

"I'm not sure I understand."

"I think perhaps you do. You surely know enough about the world we worked in, Justine as well. What do you imagine happens to people who end up knowing too much? When what they know might imperil the war effort?"

She half rose, glancing at the door.

"Justine told me nothing about her work, if that's where you're leading. She said nothing about secrets."

"This man Cabot is dangerous. I'll tell you about one of his tricks. You'll see why. It's hardly a secret. In fact, he used to boast he got it out of *Hamlet*. He would send his victims on an operation with instructions that would pretty well guarantee their capture. You see? That way you get the enemy to do the necessary."

She sat silent for a long time, immobile, pressing one hand to her cheek, her eyes dark against the pale of her face.

"You're talking about Justine, aren't you? I'm so slow."

"In my case, it was different. My operational days were over. I was simply put away. It's more effective than you might think."

"But Justine ..." Her voice was breaking, "What about Justine? What are you saying? Had she done something? God, you're not going to say you can't tell me ..."

"What had she done? Nothing at all. It was what I did. While I was in Scotland I must have written her dozens of letters. Intercepted, of course. Perhaps I wrote enough for people to assume I had talked."

"*Perhaps*? You mean you don't know? And what people? You mean this Cabot person?"

"I told Justine nothing at all. But it hardly matters. In our world you're as likely to die for a supposition as for the truth. I don't know what people will make of what I wrote. How could I?"

She stared at him, frowning, her face very pale. "Now I'm not sure I understand you. You're telling me Justine is dead. Is that what you're saying?"

"No, I'm explaining why she was so angry ... furious, you said."

"This story about you being in Paris. You mean it was a trap?"

"A trap, of course. Justine would have seen that at once. But things are never that simple. A trap needs bait. In this case, the bait is *what if it's true*? Or even, *what if it's half true*? You can see why she was angry."

"You mean ...?"

"That's the problem – I'm not sure what I mean. I have to think. If somebody wanted rid of Justine, why the elaborate plot? And why Paris? God knows, disposing of people is easy enough. Accidents happen all the time. All I know is, if John Cabot thought he had hooked another of his gullible Guildensterns, he had another think coming. Justine was one of the best agents SOE ever recruited. That's what I'm clinging to. As you say, hope is wretched stuff. Tell me, this portrait of Justine. Can I ask? It's a likeness?"

She seemed startled by the question.

"*Likeness?* I suppose it is. Why d'you ask? I don't paint portraits. But yes, in a sense ... yes it is. You would know her from it."

"I really needn't have asked. Somebody did know her. Two somebodies in fact. And one of them was John Cabot."

He stood up, stretching out his hand, "I think I'd better go. I'll write to you if I have news."

"But what are you going to do?"

"*Do*? I don't think I need do anything. You didn't hear me say this, of course, but I think I may be going to Paris."

Alex realised he had not smiled for many months, the experience was oddly invigorating. "Quite soon, I imagine."

She smiled hesitantly back, like someone not quite understanding a joke.

"Of course I'll keep all this to myself. I see very few people here. But Paris? Is that possible?"

"Well, it's true they usually don't send played out agents like me back into the field. But I'll lay odds an exception will be made. When I get back to London there'll be a letter waiting for me. Or a telephone call. Come to think of it, more likely a telephone call."

"Now you're teasing me."

He took her hand, holding until she pulled gently away.

"I can set your mind at rest about one thing. Justine is alive. I'm sure of it."

# eight

*P*ARIS. The concourse at the Gare du Nord was strangely silent. The same smell, of course: warm garlic breath mingled with gauloises cigarettes, but echoing only to the click of footsteps.

Otherwise completely quiet.

Alex stood looking round, the reason dawning. The endless feverish rattle of engines was missing.

There were no taxis.

Mounted on the pavements outside were sad lines of bicycle dogcarts touting for trade. Alex picked a contraption like a motorcycle sidecar, daringly displaying the words *Herr Himler's Stagecoach*, lowering himself onto dirty plush cushions. Asking for the rue Albéric Magnard, the man on the bicycle turned to shout, *nice day for a joker*.

He made him get out at the corner, pointing ostentatiously up the steep hill. Alex paid him off and stood for a moment, unsettled by a sense of pervasive familiarity. Paris had surely changed, but everything here was dreadfully familiar. Even the battered drainpipes against the red brickwork seemed simply to have been waiting for his return.

Tuesdays and Thursdays he took this route back from school. Every week, regular as a clock. Further to walk, but he could watch the girls playing tennis in the Park. Those were the Aunt Madeleine days, when she would greet him with soup and salad in her apartment on the Faubourg Saint Honoré.

*Rue de Franquville* stared down at him, its blue and white cartouche lower on the wall than he recalled, the battered enamel reassuringly unaltered.

Less reassuring were the new fingerposts: black metal brazenly concreted into the pavement. The closest redundantly pointed to the gates of the Ranelagh Gardens across the road, Gothic script, black on white, oddly alien. It seemed typography had secured an occupation more potent than any number of grey uniforms.

He paused for a moment at the iron gates of the park. Twenty years ago a man sold ice cream here, little boys crowding round a painted box fixed to the front of his bicycle.

A notice in German had been screwed to the metal bars: *Jews Unwanted*. The squeamish French translation underneath - *Jews are Not Admitted Here* - seemed somehow worse.

The wooden benches at the end of the gravel drive were empty. He chose one half hidden behind a statue of a man pulling something from an elaborate marble lake.

It was a terrible place for a rendezvous, the gates at the other end of the path too far for a safe escape. What sort of madman would select a place fenced on four sides? Any of a dozen windows in buildings across the road overlooked the park. Even now, someone on a tiny balcony stood looking down.

Apart from a desultory group of children sitting on the grass, the place seemed deserted. Two women pushing prams came through the gate at the apex of the long triangular walk. They seemed to be arguing. It was too far away to hear.

Alex shook a cigarette from a packet of gitanes, idly picking at threads of tobacco, leaning forward, listening. Footsteps scrunching the gravel directly behind him changed to a softer sound as someone stepped onto the grass. Someone walking fast, too close to make it safe to turn. A man tapped his shoulder, pressing lightly as Alex made to rise, holding him in his place, walking round, hand outstretched, smiling.

Younger than Alex imagined, a thin lugubrious face, unshaven, his suit a wide pin-stripe that had seen better days. The sort you saw haunting the market, selling watches. The wire-framed spectacles could not have been his own.

"It is a fisherman." Paris accent. He slumped down next to Alex, legs stretched out, breathing heavily as if the walk had been too much for him.

"It's supposed to be a fisherman catching the head of Orpheus in his net. There's a description on the other side."

He tugged at Alex's arm, trying to pull him up, the gesture too friendly. "D'you want to see?"

Freeing himself, Alex walked to where the flowerbeds were set off with little metal hoops. Things had not started well. The place was bad enough, but pointless familiarity was going to kill them both.

He turned to face him, speaking quietly into his face.

"You are Jules, right? *Jules?*"

The smile when it arrived was not pleasant, a kind of sneering concession.

"Ah yes, of course. I was told." He gave a weary little bow. "Captain Vere will be formal, they said." He scraped a line in the gravel with one foot, darting behind it like a fencer, a childish comic gesture.

"*And you, Alex*? I am correct, eh? Or do we fight?"

Alex stepped back, feeling foolish.

A German soldier in dress uniform turned in through the gate. He seemed too fat for the girl at his side, one chubby arm barely stretching round her waist. Seeing men standing at the statue, the girl pulled him away, the two of them taking the other path, talking quietly together, her head tipped up to his. They seemed an unlikely couple.

The voice of the man at Alex's side merged with their distant whispered conversation: "Paris is for lovers, is it not?" You could smell tobacco on his breath. "Best not to look. We will startle them. Let's sit. We are quite safe. Rue Saint André des Arts. You know it?"

"In the sixth? Vaguely. I can find it."

"Come through the Place Saint-Michel. The house is Number 32, it's on the left. Eight o'clock tonight. Paris keeps Berlin time now - you will remember that?" He reached for Alex's hand, "Eight precise. You understand the word *precise*?"

Alex jerked his hand away, "For Christ's sake ..."

"The time is important."

"I'll be there."

But the man was already walking away, pausing only to light a cigarette at the gates.


The absurd charade in the Ranelagh Gardens had been Major Elton's idea. Maurice Elton, his rank unchanged, flexing London muscles, settled behind the final utility desk of his career.

A modest adjustment to his security clearance had served only to change the colour of files that filled his days.

Two nondescript men in raincoats had met the night train from Dundee at King's Cross. Standing next to the newspaper stand, inquisitive eyes had settled on Alex before he reached the barrier. They waited as he searched for his ticket, standing politely to one side while he read their warrant cards.

A car was waiting outside. You would hardly call it an arrest.

The meeting in Coram Street later that morning brought memories of the interminable days spent with Cabot manufacturing lies for the TPSU. Yet another requisitioned room in some anonymous Bloomsbury flat smelling vaguely of cats.

The windows were pasted over with strips of paper throwing faint bars of sunlight across the wallpaper.

Perhaps England's war was always going to be like this – sweating, anxious men crammed into unsuitable places. Improvising.

They were three: a silent anonymous man perched next to Alex, huge shoes spoiling someone's abandoned carpets, the two of them on borrowed chairs, their knees almost touching. And Elton: safely behind his desk, curiously emboldened by a new London veneer. Elton playing spies, there to do his masters' bidding, whether he knew it or not.

During those interminable months at Torridon, Alex had dispensed only one certain truth to the agents in his command: *Gullible people for the most part know they are gullible.* He considered it a personal discovery. Certainly, psychology offered no explanation for the strange social alchemy that obliges the gulled to acquiesce in their own downfall.

It was obvious to all three that Alex was being set up: equally obvious that he would acquiesce. Watching Elton's mouth move, he had the impression he was attending a kind of demonstration.

He heard him out in rising fury, thinking of Justine's Dundee visitors, barely bothering to listen to the stream of disingenuous velvet words, thinking only how puerile it all sounded.

"It sounds complicated." Alex had become conscious Elton was waiting for a response. He blurted the words out - they were the best he could do. "Complicate things you end up with a cockup. I should know, I've been in enough."

Elton looked pained, "I can't agree. This is Paris we're talking about, not your rural stomping ground. It's all a question of allegiances. In Paris they shift by the hour, if half of what I hear is true." He leaned forward, "We're not all that sure whose side this Cabot chap thinks he's on."

He tapped a bulky anonymous folder as if Cabot himself might be folded inside, "You'll need to tread carefully if you're to trace him. But you know that. You worked with him. Canny's the word."

"Oh, that's the word, alright. Cabot runs rings round most people." Watching Elton's face, secretly smug, Alex suddenly understood what he was up to. The fool must have chased up Cabot's name after that interview in Torridon. Must have discovered he was alive, after all. Incredibly, he'd set himself to second guess John Cabot. Perhaps there was some satisfaction in knowing the inevitable outcome. All the same, demeaning to be played by someone like Elton. But it was not impossible Justine might be in Paris. That was the hell of it – not completely impossible. Alex imagined Cabot was staring at him, reading his expression. He smiled back: "What's he supposed to have done? I'm tempted to say, *what else*? You realise, I'll need to know if I'm to haul him back to mother in chains."

Elton's laugh, when it came, was not particularly convincing. "You weren't listening, Alex. No question of chains, or hauling for that matter. We just want you to find him. You're a godsend to us. Nobody in Paris knows him from Adam. He was a civil servant, not an agent. You know him by sight – that's why we need you."

"Why's he there? What's he up to?"

Elton glanced nervously down at the folder, "We don't know."

The silent man at Alex's side stirred briefly, nodding approvingly at the *we*.

"We don't even know how he got there? Any ideas?"

"Don't look at me. Until a few weeks ago I didn't think he was going anywhere, I thought he was dead. Remember?"

"Yes, I remember your telling me that. You do realise nobody at Torridon knew he was behind your … your …?"

"*Consigne?* Or would you prefer *incarceration?*"

"A bit strong, but if you like. Look, the fellow misled us. Unfortunate …"

Elton had a habit of talking himself into a dead end. He looked unhappily at the end of his pencil.

"But you've got the wrong end of the stick. We don't want him back." He darted a glance at the other man, "Strictly speaking, he's nothing to do with Intelligence. It's true he worked for London Controlling Section, but that's over."

"Sacked was he? Blotted his copy book? Or did somebody actually take the trouble to find out what he was up to all those days in the TPSU? Are you sure nobody's decided the reclusive Mr C is best out of the way? One-way trips have been arranged before."

"Look Alex, we appreciate you don't like him - no, don't say anything - and I can appreciate your reasons. Don't you think you might be getting things out of proportion? Let's leave it I've set myself to find out what Cabot's up to in Paris. My *consigne*, if you like." The fleeting smile at his little joke was unwisely superior, "and all things considered, you seem to be best placed to find him." He risked a tiny theatrical intake of breath before tossing Alex the bait. "Besides, it's your chance to turn the tables on him. You realise that?"

"How's that?"

"What we thought was ... well ... it was your Mr Cabot ordered that *sine contactu* regarding that woman. Are you still looking for her? He must know where she is. Here's your chance to find out."

Alex stared venomously back at him, fuming. "Her name's Perry."

Elton had relaxed, hanging onto his smile, knowing the game was won. He opened the slim folder in front of him.

"Now ... liaison. I know it's clumsy, but we're stuck with intermediaries. No need to frown like that, this lot are alright. Paris is full of amateurs now."

"I'll take your word for it. All the same, why not forget the spy games. It shouldn't be all that difficult if I have the right papers. I can't see we have to involve the frogs at all."

"Can't be done, Alex. They say they want to look at you first. Resistance in Paris has been a bit passive up to now. Open city and all that, you know. But not much longer. It's changing. You could find yourself in a shooting war."

The man at Alex's side had stifled a snigger at *passive*. He squirmed restlessly in his chair. The trap sprung, he had lost interest. Plainly, he wanted to go home.

"So I'm expected to wander round Paris in broad daylight, trading passwords with someone you hope isn't an amateur. You did look at my file, didn't you, Maurice? I've been captured twice in France. Open city or not, when I last checked, Paris was under occupation. How long do you think I'm going to last?"

The silence was painful, all of them suddenly conscious of faint sounds from the street outside.

*A day. Perhaps two. Not longer.*

"There's milice informers everywhere, Alex."

Elton was getting his second wind, relishing this role as commissioner of operations, "That's why the French insist on seeing you. Slip up over that and we'll be walking you into a trap."

Something in Alex's face made him look away, leaving the words hanging in the quiet room. Elton stared defiantly at a picture on the other wall, one hand nervily playing with his bundle of papers.

Alex felt suddenly light-headed, conscious of entering a kind of *folie à deux*.

"Walk me into a trap. Perish the thought."

"We're relying on the Yanks to get you into Paris." Elton's expression was uncertain. "There's a briefing about that this afternoon."

He found another page in the bundle of papers, running his finger along a line. "You're to make contact in a place called Ranelagh Gardens. A chap by the name of Jules."

"*Ranelagh Gardens.*" Elton let out an awkward bark of a laugh. "Let's hope they don't mean the ones in Chelsea! You can look it up in the Map Room. It's in the sixteenth arrondissement."

"I don't need to look it up. I know where it is."

"Of course you do, I was forgetting. You know Paris, don't you? Right."

He leaned forward, passing Alex a sheet of paper. "The gen's all there. Baker Street sorted it out. You trade names as a pass phrase with the bloke in the Gardens. He'll give you the address of the circuit. You'll have to see what leads they have on Cabot. The problem is nobody knows what he looks like. Last we heard he was too close for comfort to the Vichy lot. Shouldn't be too hard to find."

Remembering something, he waved at the paper. "Your safe house is in there. Make for that if things go awry."

"What is there to go awry?"

"Nothing, nothing at all - just the usual fall back."

Alex stared blankly at the bit of paper.

The man at his side was already making for the door.

# nine

IT was just past seven when he reached the Place Saint-Michel. When he was a boy, *L'Auberge de la Place* commanded one side of the square, looking across to the fountain and beyond to the narrow twists of the rue Saint André des Arts.

Close enough, but not suicidally close.

Years ago Alex would weave his way between noisy tables right here, warm summer evenings reeking of aniseed and perfume, women leaning out to ruffle his hair as he hurried past, tugging at him to see the books he was carrying. An awestruck schoolboy late from class, hurrying to his Aunt Madeleine's.


Elton had been right about one thing: Paris had changed. *L'Auberge de la Place* had disappeared, war shrivelling it to nothing. Even the name had gone, leaving *Le Coq d'Or* scrawled in white paint across a single shabby glass door. Inside, lines of polished brass pumps on the long mahogany bar were all that remained of the old *Auberge*.

Albeit summer, the place was cold, everywhere the inescapable smell of bad drains. A reedy wireless bleated high up from over the door, a woman singing.

Alex laid a coin on the bar, waiting for the stubby glass of red wine to appear alongside. The tables were empty: you stood to drink at this time of night, scurrying home to listen to the news.

It was a quarter to eight.

Through a side window he could see an old man cleaning out a handcart on the corner of the rue Saint André des Arts, half climbing onto the boards, flicking bits of cabbage stalk down into the gutter. Two men in a shop doorway watched indulgently from the other side of the street, trading jokes, reluctantly breaking apart now and then as people pushed by.

A boy running down the narrow street found his feet skidding on fresh green leaves. He grabbed the handle of the cart, swaying to steady himself. Suddenly alert, one of the men stepped out onto the pavement, brusquely hauling the boy up, pushing him on his way.

The barman filled Alex's empty glass, exchanging the coin for a pile of copper, nodding as Alex left it lying there.

He carried the drink to a table by the door, opening an abandoned copy of *Soir*, letting street sounds orchestrate his glances outside.

A girl in a short white coat came out of the *Pharmacie* on the corner, gesticulating to someone inside until an illuminated sign went out.

The old man began pushing his empty cart up the street, slowly disappearing from view.

The wireless over the door fell silent.

It was eight o'clock.

A double whistle sounded from somewhere far away, barely audible. The kind used to control traffic, when there was traffic to control. Another - much closer. Close enough to bring the barman from behind his counter, pulling the street door open, stepping out onto the pavement, still polishing a glass with a white cloth.

Alex lowered the newspaper. The two men in the doorway had disappeared. Then he saw them. Further up the street, side by side among the cabbage stalks, pistols drawn.

Frightened women with prams hurried past, trying not to look.

The barman came back inside, pushing his glass hard against an upturned bottle of Pastis behind the bar. He topped it up from the water jug, glancing across to Alex.

"Fucking milice."

Alex folded the paper back to the race results.

A little crowd had gathered outside, moodily silent, splitting into two as a car, one door hanging open, backed the wrong way down the rue Saint André des Arts. A Gendarme jumped out, hanging on while the car slewed across the pavement, skidding to a halt. He walked to join the two men. They stood in line abreast, drowning in a stream of bicycles and perambulators.

The vegetable cart inched its way back, looking for somewhere flat to park, the old man kneeling to slip a wedge under the wheels. Failing to haul himself up, he gave in, sitting where he was, letting the crowd pick its way over his splayed legs.

A slight anonymous figure followed the stragglers down into the square, sauntering slowly, smoking a cigarette. The same shabby pin-stripe suit, although he had abandoned the wire-frame spectacles. Seeing the Gendarme, he walked slowly across to shake hands, the two of them standing silently, gazing up the street. As they climbed back into the car they were sharing a joke.


It was getting on for nine when Alex left the *Coq*, walking across the silent bridge into the embracing twilight on the other side of the river. He had watched the car disappear into the maze of streets beyond the square. It would have been tempting to follow, but he was in no mood for temptation.

Soon enough – perhaps already - someone in London would know that Captain Vere had refused the bait.

A few men had drifted into the bar after the raid, nervously eyeing each other, drinking in silence. Alex had sat on, nursing the glass of wine, remembering Inverness. Remembering Elton. Wondering what came next.

As betrayals went, the affair seemed dangerously inconsequential. Perhaps the man in the park had guessed the cautious Captain Vere would find it all too obvious.

*In which case, why?*

He finished his drink and stood up, nodding to the barman. Elton's orders had been to make for the safe house. One thing was certain: wherever else he went tonight, it would not be within a mile of that place. In truth, he had settled that hours ago, even before he reached the Place Saint-Michel. For him, there was only one safe place in Paris. And that was somewhere neither Elton nor Cabot even knew existed.


At the top of the rue du Temple, three men were closing up a battered removal van, gas bottles strapped to its roof. Alex crossed to the other pavement, not risking his accent on a pointless greeting. They seemed in no mood for bonhomie in any case, sullenly waiting until he had reached the corner before banging the van doors closed. He heard them drive away.

It was quieter here, a few passers-by hurrying to beat the nine o'clock curfew. Late evening sun coloured the upper stories of the buildings pink. He glanced back down the gloom of the empty street. It seemed unlikely he was followed, but he was in no mood for risks either. He slipped quietly into the stone portico of some municipal office, pressing into the shade, his back hard against the door. Ten minutes by his watch: an agony of time. No following footsteps. Nothing but grey tenements quietly dissolving into the gathering dark.

Aunt Madeleine's gallery was in the old Jewish quarter. A double frontage next to a place that mended clocks in the rue Gravilliers. Every Wednesday, because school ended early and Aunt Madeleine was busy, he would go to the gallery for lunch. How long had he done that? Hard to remember: it seemed forever.

All he could recall was a burly man in a leather apron, always carrying something. He tried to remember his name, but it wouldn't come. But his wife was called Sophie. A tall excitable woman who watched him eat, endlessly chattering - she would remember him, he was sure of it.

At the corner it seemed he had mistaken the way. The rue Gravilliers was always crowded. The shops were supposed to close, although somehow they never did. Even at night the place was crammed. A war would hardly change all that. He remembered squeezing past crowds to reach the gallery door, remembered walking home head-down past the first of the street girls, scared to see they were little older than himself. Sometimes they would stand in threes and fours, calling out as he scuttled past.

There was no one calling now. Apart from roaming cats, the whole of the narrow cobbled street was silent and deserted.

Aunt Madeleine's gallery had been boarded up, rough planks brutally nailed into the ornate carving. The huge double doors at the side were locked, a notice pinned to the little inset door: *Sealed on the Orders of The Prefecture of Paris*. The date was impossible to make out.

An odd arrangement of steel wire was stapled to the frame of the door, running round the metal catch, ending in a lead seal. Someone had cut the wire. The little door stood pushed in. Alex peered inside, a rotten smell of piss and abandonment blowing past him. A single gas lamp under a tin shade threw sickly yellow light onto rows of post boxes stuffed with neglected newspapers, limp with damp.

The Concierge's lean-to cell was deserted, a single broken chair lying on its side inside. A square of card had been pinned to the bottom pane of the window. He could read it from where he stood.

*Gone away.*


It took half an hour to reach Aunt Madeleine's apartment on the Faubourg Saint Honoré, walking faster than he should, barely controlling an obscure rising panic. He had been prepared for Sophie offering him that blank look that declared ancient acquaintance far too dangerous to acknowledge - but hardly prepared for the gallery simply disappearing, wiped out, along with the rest of the street.

Paris had changed, true enough.

He threaded an anxious way through streets he had forgotten he knew. Already past nine, the restaurants were still crowded. Caught up in the crowd spilling out from a cinema, he found himself walking alongside a solitary German soldier. Almost too young to be in uniform, the man was limping heavily, leaning on a stick. He stopped to let people push past, stepping down into the road, ceding them their pavement. Alex glanced at him, their eyes met briefly: two men exchanging frightened glances, hurrying by.

The apartment on the second floor had acquired a freshly painted door. He stood erect in front of the glass bead of a spy hole, stoically composing his face against the possibility that she had long since moved, was dead even.

The door opened almost too soon to his knock, an elegant woman in a cloche hat holding it against the chain peering through the crack, her face the sketch of someone he once had known. In his school days Aunt Madeleine had been unimaginably old. This elegant woman seemed barely his senior. She released the chain, pulling the door back, standing a long minute on the threshold surveying him.

"Aunt Madeleine," awkwardly extending his hand, "it's Alex ... d'you ...?"

She surged forward, filling the marble hallway with a cloud of perfume.

"Heavens above! Yes, Alexandre. It is, isn't it? God in heaven!"

There was an odd pre-war flavour to her English, the accent slightly stilted. She sounded a little like his mother. She went on tapping her breast in surprise.

"You're alone? Yes, yes, of course you're alone. Why would you not be?" She frowned at a tiny watch on her wrist, pursing her lips in

73

an exaggerated look of despair. "And I was on my way out. I'm late ... I'm always late. But come in ... come in."

He let her pull him by one hand into the lighted hallway, leaving the door behind them open.

Little had changed. Persian carpets dotted an expanse of ancient parquet; the same two gilt-framed mirrors silently faced each other across the hall. A Chinese bowl of freesias on the little rosewood table spilled a cold scent into the air.

There were pictures everywhere, the walls crammed with canvasses. He was a schoolboy again, late for supper, satchel laced at his back, staring wide-eyed at more painted flesh than his thoughts could contain. Splayed legs, sprawling thighs like butcher's meat, terrifying pendulous breasts, nipples jutting red: everything too close, inexpressibly strange, the only common theme a kind of sophisticated menace.

She stood close to the mirror adjusting her lipstick, eyeing his reflection in the glass, one hand flailing behind for her handbag.

As he rescued it for her, she turned and drew him close, exchanging kisses, left and right, laughing as he reared back to avoid the inevitable third.

She was digging fruitlessly into her bag. "Damn. I've left my case somewhere. Can you give me a cigarette? I assume you come armed with American cigarettes? It's alright, I know better than to ask questions."

Alex lit a cigarette for her, watching as she drew on it, her eyes widening. She exhaled a thin mist of smoke. "Terrible to say, but I needed that. My word, you choose your time. You are a dreadful shock, my dear boy. A good shock. When was it last? Just before this damned war. Now you make me think it really is ending. You're not the first, you know." Suddenly pressing her fingers to her lips like a child regretting a secret betrayed, "There, I'm saying too much. But you will know all that. Paris is waking up."

She waved a gloved hand to the glazed door opening onto the salon. "You know where to go. I will be an hour, no more. You can bear that? I have a rendezvous … impossible to re-arrange. My telephone has ceased to function again. It is always in that state now. *Paris*. Have you eaten? Are you a modern man - can you make an omelette? There are eggs in the kitchen. You can take two. You can find your room? Nothing has changed. I still think of the bedroom upstairs as little Alexandre's."

She was already past the doorway, calling over her shoulder, "I will take the stairs - the lift is too slow. I've a new girl. She'll be back very late – no one seems to care about the curfew any more. I don't trust these girls – heaven only knows who she'll be writing to when she finds there's a man here."

Her voice echoed up the marble staircase.

"Make yourself at home. There's drinks, just look. And eat something, you look starved."

A distant door below clicked onto silence.


There was a whisky decanter on the side table in the salon. Alex poured himself a drink. Beyond the window, Paris without its traffic exhaled an eerie silence.

Madeleine gone, everywhere seemed unnaturally quiet. He drew the curtains back and stepped onto the little balcony, the scent of lime trees rising out of the warm dark to greet him. In the street below leisurely footsteps shuffled past, couples arm in arm, their voices no more than a murmur.

For the first time in many weeks he felt safe.

A tiny metal table was still set with breakfast things, presumably waiting on the maid Madeleine could not quite trust. He slumped into the chair, pushing a coffee cup aside, staring sightlessly over the grey clutter of leaded rooftops to the distant horizon, the Paris skyline etched black against the last bloody streaks of sunset.

A familiar obsessive incantation welled into his consciousness: thoughts of Justine. Even now, she could be watching this same darkening sky, perhaps not so many yards from here.

She was here in Paris – he was certain of it.

Calculations that had consumed him since Dundee wormed back into his mind. Five months pregnant in May: that must be so. Her baby would be an October child. Perhaps there was consolation in that: October was Alex's month.

A sudden cessation of the street sounds below brought him to his feet, staring dumbly into the silence, the memory of Major Gliess a pain even now he dared not acknowledge.

He turned to look into the lighted room, his back against the balcony rail. Nothing had changed. Furnished long before another war, the present war had left its shabby charm untouched. How many times had schoolboy Alex stood awestruck in the quiet intimacy of that elegant room, Aunt Madeleine's greeting unfailingly the same? Today, her smile at the door had effortlessly erased the intervening years. It was as if he had never been away, as if she had been expecting him.

Already a pulse was jerking painfully in his neck, a sudden tension gripping his heart. There was no doubt about it: she had been expecting him.

# ten

FOR the second time that day he stood frozen, battling a rising surge of panic. He had been right: it had all seemed too obvious. Thinking to escape two traps, he had blithely hurried himself into the only one that mattered.

He had given lectures at Torridon on response to extreme stress, on the tendency to find sinister purpose in the inconsequential. One afternoon, on a whim, playing the good psychologist, he had given it an ironic name: *Agent's Paranoia*. Always good for a ripple of polite laughter.

Rotating his head to free the knot of pain in his neck, he forced his breathing into a textbook pattern, counting aloud on the exhale, trying to clear his mind, conscious only of danger, imminent and deadly, hearing his own voice floating thin and pointless onto the warm Paris air.

He stepped back into the salon, at once feeling naked in the light of the room, snatching the curtains closed at his back.

*She had been expecting him.*

If that were true, he was lost. So much for psychology: it was his turn to realise lectures rarely counted for much. How little anyone truly knew of paranoia. He had read the books: it was impossible for the subject to determine the truth of his own state. He had read the books: he never imagined the subject would be himself.

*The paranoid imagine they are spied on.*

What use telling that to a spy whose whole life is lived with spies?

*The paranoid believe they are plotted against.*

What use knowing that when your whole life has been lived in a hall of mirrors, bluff and counter-bluff endlessly reflecting themselves?

*The paranoid falsely believe they are sincerely loved.*

What use talking of erotomania to someone lost to love? To someone wagering his life for the only woman he would ever love? For a woman who may not even be alive?

He walked out into the hall, his footsteps seeming unnaturally loud on the polished parquet.

The rucksack lay on the floor where Madeleine had tossed it under a chair, her careless gesture now dreadfully imbued with some other purpose.

Kneeling down, he fumbled at the straps, frantically plunging his hand inside, feeling for the touch of the metal cold against his hand. Thank god: still there.

He pulled the Model B out, turning it in his hand, seeing it for what it was, slowly unwinding the suppressor. Surely too late to fret about noise? It was a reassurance, all the same, that pistol. What was it she had said? *Armed with American cigarettes.* Perhaps she believed he had dared not risk a pistol, walking the streets.

He slumped down, legs outstretched, his back against the wall, feeling sweat rise hot along the line of his spine, trying to take stock, waiting for an odd light-headedness to pass, his mind invaded by a kind of sick hopelessness. The light above his head was too bright, the hall too exposed. Everywhere was too exposed.

The business in the rue Saint André des Arts must have unsettled him more than he realised. That, and the endless wait in the *Coq d'Or*. The day's pointless betrayals had had Cabot's fingerprints on them – he was sure of it. But surely Cabot could not have known an inconspicuous schoolboy decades ago had a habit of visiting his aunt after school? No one could possibly have known Alex would end up here.

A slight draught across the hall came cold on his face flushed suddenly with relief. He found himself smiling into space like an idiot, grateful Aunt Madeleine was late, that she had not come back to find some madman waving a pistol at her.

Obviously, he had been wrong, fallen victim to some curious kind of recursive paranoia. Madeleine could not possibly have been expecting him. He was letting Cabot loom too large, letting him infect his thoughts. No one could have predicted his coming here, least of all Cabot. He had only made the decision himself an hour ago. To predict that would take somebody who knew him better than he knew himself.

It was only as he hauled himself up into a chair, the pistol still in his hand, that the true nature of his gullibility struck, turning his stomach.

He had forgotten that bulging file with its pink sticker.

Captain Alex Vere's whole life was in that file. You had only to trawl through it to see what might lead him here. *In extremis*, where else would he come? The address in the Faubourg Saint Honoré would be there. Buried, but certainly there. You would find it if you were persistent.

And John Cabot was nothing if not persistent.

The more he thought on it, the more cunning this final betrayal seemed. Aunt Madeleine need know nothing of it. All that was called for were calculated steps to bring him here, and those had been effortlessly achieved. She need only return with whoever they chose. A car and two or three men – that was all it would take. And his charming reliable aunt would have innocently delivered him hog-tied to his death. Nothing theatrical, nothing elaborate. This elegant apartment would make for a quiet arrest and it was safe to assume the gullible victim would wait. After all, he had been complicit from the start. She might even apologise as they led him away.

He barely had the strength to stand. Hunger, stress, fatigue, fear - all of them – had sapped what spirit was left. Glistening beads of sweat made the smooth metal of the pistol wet. He had never known his hands to sweat like this. It seemed he was terribly unwell, too far gone to plan.

He looked down at the weapon in his lap, vacantly registering that the safety flip was down. *You die for mistakes like that.* In some distant Torridon life he had been fond of that pompous phrase. How they must have tired of it. He watched a disinterested finger resting on the catch, already knowing he would never fire the thing. Whatever had corrupted her was not worth her life - it was barely worth his own. Anyway, only a madman would try to shoot his way out of a second-floor flat. He would be arrested here. He would sit and wait.

When it came to it, his only regret was that Justine would never know.

She was late. Steadying himself against the wall, he tried to focus on the face of his watch, the image of the glass rippling in time with waves of gagging nausea, everything oddly blurred. An hour, she had said. She was very late. No, *they* were late. It was just a matter of how many. And something else she had said - her telephone didn't work.

It came to him uncalled, another childish Torridon rule: *always check.*

He walked unsteadily down the narrow corridor to the study, surprised to remember the way.

She had left the light on. It was hard to imagine she spent much time in this forlorn little room smelling faintly of furniture polish. Files were piled neatly on a desk facing the window, the telephone alongside, perched on a little stand.

He heard the dialling tone even as he lifted the receiver from its cradle.

Her diary lay flung open, a huge affair in green morocco, a silver pencil lodged in the crease. He switched on the desk light, flipping the pages apart. Aunt Madeleine was not unoccupied. Every hour, it seemed, was filled with names, times, telephone numbers. Nothing in particular against today. No scrawl of *Alex*. Nothing either that might be a plausible code. But then, she hardly need remind herself.

There was a stack of thin manila folders on the desk. He picked one up, labelled *Bassano* in Madeleine's handwriting. Inside, nothing but typed pages, cataloguing paintings, columns listing title, size, medium, date, painter - annotations inked in the margin here and there in the same irregular scrawl. The folders underneath were bulkier, one labelled *Lévitan*, the other *Austerlitz*, twenty or thirty typed pages in each, in the same style: title, size, medium, date, painter.

But for the names, it seemed no more than an inventory of stock.

*But for the names.*

He found himself wildly scanning the room, searching for something that would do, *anything* that would do, a sudden scald of bile burning his throat. He was too late. He kneeled over the wicker basket, yellow vomit pooling over crumpled paper, liquid leaking round his knees. Everywhere, the stink of sour red wine.


The door to the gallery along the hall was not locked. Years ago, visits here had been a rare concession. It had been a vast unfurnished room, bare white walls showing two or three canvasses, rarely more, sometimes only one.

A flat fug of stale air greeted him, the windows shuttered and closed. The switch at the door threw stark yellow light onto dozens of heavy gilt frames jostling for space, a confused jumble rising to the ceiling.

White luggage labels dangled down, completed in the same impatient scrawl: Degas, Dufy, Sisley, Manet, Pissarro, van Gogh, Monet, Rouart. They were not displayed so much as hoarded there: the indiscriminate collection of some obsessive madman wealthy beyond imagination.

The door swung back, revealing other paintings hidden behind. A brutal display of afterthoughts hung with no other thought but suspension, their faces to the wall. Stark bare canvasses on wooden stretchers, luggage labels dangling down, names swinging as the door clicked shut: Braque, Severini, Miro, Picasso, Chagall.

A painting was propped on a wooden easel in the centre of the gallery, covered with a dust sheet. Pulling at it, Alex found himself uncomfortably close to a little girl. Or, rather, a miniature adult framed in gold, its profiled figure too old for its years. A blue ribbon perched awkwardly in her hair, the ends falling away like the forked tail of some exotic fish. Her hands were placidly clasped in her lap, sophisticated eyes fixing something beyond the frame, seeing more than they ought.

A metal plate let into the frame was engraved with the single word: *Bassano*.

Alex found the signature at last, lost in a mass of green vegetation high on the right, the letters not quite straight: *r e n o i r*. There was no label.

"*Here you are, then*. I was looking for you everywhere. What do you think? You think it's a copy?"

Madeleine was looking at him, her hair a little awry, standing at the open door, fighting to catch her breath. She pulled the coat from her shoulders, letting it fall onto a chair, startled eyes fixing the pistol in his hand.

"Alexandre, why are you in here? What's the matter?"

He gestured her to move from the door, straining to see beyond into the empty hall. She seemed to have come alone. Whoever had brought her must be waiting in the street below.

She had dropped into a chair, nervously watching him walk to the door, her expression impossible to read.

"You look ill, my dear. Have you eaten? Can you put that gun away, it frightens me. God, Alexandre, where are you going? Come back. You can't walk the streets at this time of night. Not in that state. Don't you realise if you're found with a gun …?"

He looked up, searching for her eyes, her face oddly blurred.

"Do you know why I came here?"

She frowned, slowly shaking her head. "Well, no, not really. I expected you would say. There have been many mysterious visitors lately ... we call them *visitors* ... you are not the first."

"Just listen to me, for God's sake. I came because I thought I'd be safe. Can you possibly know what it feels like to find somebody you trust ... to find somebody you trusted ... sells you out. And for what? No, I've a better question. *Why*?"

"Sell you? What on earth are you talking about? If you came here to shoot me, for heaven's sake get on with it. Do you think I care? Please put your ridiculous gun down."

"How many are there down there waiting? At least tell me that. It would cost you nothing."

"Ah, you mean there are people looking for you. I knew it would be something like that. No, you are safe. Nobody was there when I came back. I am late. I waited for Stephanie outside the cinema until they switched the street lights off. The stupid girl shouldn't be out at this time of night, she'll get herself arrested. I was going to walk back with her. She wasn't there ... some man I suppose. Do sit down, Alexandre. You look really dreadful. I think you are ill. I'll go down again and see. If that's what you want?"

"You seriously think I'd let you do that? I'm not mad."

"Actually I think you are. At the moment ... a little mad. Go and look for yourself if you like."

She sat impassively, waiting for him to move, one hand plucking at her glove.

"Do stop being like this, Alexandre. It begins to frighten me. Here, I've thought of something. You can see the street from the balcony in the salon."

She sprang up, standing alongside him, pulling at him, her arms round a dead weight. "Here we go, there's good boy. We'll both go and look."

At the touch of her hand he sank down to his knees, pressing the floor to steady himself, the room suddenly darker, closing in. It seemed there was little more to see than a patch of wood at the foot of the easel. His hands sank into the spongy mass of the parquet, watching his pistol slide away, skidding over the floor. The foot of the easel rose up to meet him, his forehead dissolving into it.

Somewhere at the far edge of consciousness he remembered the yawning silence that precedes catastrophe, something huge embracing him. A momentary awareness of the surprising weight of glass. Shards of inflexible pain. Terrible pain. Then nothing. Nothing at all.

# eleven

THE rattle of wooden curtain hoops filled the room with bright sunlight, a tiny breeze scented with lime carrying the murmur of street sounds into the room.

A huge chamber pot, decorated with green and yellow dandelions, loomed over him, perched on top of the wooden *chevet* at his bedside.

Madeleine twisted the handle towards him.

"We thought you might need it in the night. More effective than a wicker basket. How do you feel this morning? You slept a long time."

Alex pushed himself up in the bed, wincing as the pillow snagged his neck, staring round, "How did I get in here?"

"Well, that was quite difficult. You have Stephanie to thank. She is stronger than I thought. You can also thank her for the bandage. It hurts?"

"No. Well, yes ... it doesn't matter. Stephanie? I remember you coming back alone. In the gallery. Is that right?"

Sunlight across the bed hurt his eyes, confused fragments of yesterday clamouring for attention. He knew where he was, there was that much to be thankful for, but how he got here remained uncertain.

"I think I must have fainted. I remember I'd been thinking about Doctor Clérambault. Odd to remember that."

"Actually, you seemed to be thinking about a gun. Have you forgotten?" She went to the window, fiddling with the cord of the blinds, her back to him.

"This doctor. Someone in Paris? I've never heard of him."

"No, nothing like that. He was a psychiatrist, somebody I'd read about. I was a student of psychology before the war. Perhaps you knew?"

"No. Why would I know that? I can't believe you came to Paris to see this doctor."

"No, no, he's long dead. Committed suicide, in fact. He wrote a lot about manias."

She frowned. "So you decided to bring your *manias* here?" As she turned round he saw his pistol dangling awkwardly from her finger.

"And does your dead doctor explain this?"

"Christ! Be careful! Let me see that thing."

"I think not. When I returned home it was pointing at me."

She laid it carefully on the table in front of the window, "There is really no call to explain, Alexandre. At least not everything. I can guess why you are here. You are not my first, you know. I told you - Paris is filled with visitors."

Her smile stripped him of years. She was Aunt Madeleine again, climbing the stairs to his little upstairs bedroom, standing at his bedside as he drank his special morning chocolate.

"The pistol … be careful."

"Stephanie made it safe. I could have done it myself, but it was entertaining to watch her. I was surprised she knew such a thing. I suppose it's the company she keeps. Well, you are here. Am I to know why?"

She waited for him to speak, her eyebrows framing the question.

"Why I'm here? I was almost arrested yesterday. They had set a trap for me. Then it seemed coming here was part of another trap. I was not thinking very well. I convinced myself you were somehow part of the mess."

"*Me*? What has your arrest to do with me?"

"Nothing. I'm sorry. It is sometimes hard to be rational. Betrayal has curious effects on the psyche. If it happens too many times you can become a little mad. It's as if you have nowhere solid to stand. It's hard to explain - you have to experience it to know ..."

"So you think I've not experienced it?" Her voice was suddenly hard. "You can't know much about Paris. Paris is nothing but betrayal. I will say I am sorry for you, if that's what you want. Now are you going to say why you are really here? No more nonsense about doctors. Or is it a secret?"

"No, not a secret. I was sent to contact someone. A man. Now I start to doubt he's here. Perhaps he's not involved at all. All I know is somebody wants me out of the way, both of us out of the way ..." He stumbled into silence. .

She came and sat on the little chair at his bedside, waiting until their eyes met.

"Both of you? So there is more to say. You forget, I know you. I remember when little Alexandre looked like that. Perhaps this man was not the only reason."

"Yes, there's another reason. A woman. Someone I worked with a long time ago. I was looking for a woman."

"*Was*? You mean you have found her?"

"Oh, no: the reverse. After yesterday I realise she was just the bait to get me here. She's probably not even in Paris. That's why I woke up thinking about that dead doctor, as you call him. He wrote about people who waste their whole life looking for somebody. I'll never find her – I find that hard to accept. It's a kind of madness."

"Yes, you looked a little mad. But this woman: did she have a name? That can't be a secret."

"Her name is Justine Perry."

"I like the name. French?"

"She spent most of her life in France." Something in Madeleine's expression drew the words from him: "And something else. There's a child. She has a child."

"Ah, Alexandre, this is a very French story. And this is your child? A little boy? Somehow I think of a little boy."

Seeing the pity in her eyes, Alex was suddenly consumed by a kind of weary resentment.

She reached out, patting his arm like a patient nurse, managing a brittle little smile, "Yes, you're right. Perhaps not now. I'll go and make us some coffee. Stephanie brought you some very early, but she left you to sleep. I will fetch your clothes. She did what she could with them. There was blood."

"I forgot. I should have told you. Last night, before you got back. I was in your office."

She stood up, making for the door, laughing, "Oh, we discovered that! But why were you in there?"

"The telephone - you said it wasn't working."

"Did I? It works now I think." She whirled round, her eyes wide with alarm, "God, you didn't use it? Oh, no! What is it you've brought down on me? You really are mad!"

"Of course I didn't use it. I'm not that mad."

"Aren't you? I remember what you said when I got back last night? Have you forgotten?"

"I'm not sure. Did I say I thought somebody was using you as bait for a trap? It's not as strange as it sounds, that's how these people work. They used Justine to lure me to Paris."

"*Lure you*? That sounds very dramatic."

"If you like. War is dramatic. I realised they would work out I would come here. It made me think you were involved."

"Involved to do what? Anybody would guess you would come here. Where else would you come running? You were always a very transparent boy, Alexandre."

She came back to the little chair, pulling it closer to the bed, the hospital visitor wondering how best to put something.

"Let me tell you about the meeting I went to last night. I think it might concern you …"

"So there really was a meeting?"

She pursed he lips, suddenly impatient.

"Are you always so suspicious? Why would I bother to lie about that? People of the *Quartier*. We talk about the future, about whether we have one. It's all we can do to stay sane. You have no idea - Paris is like a madhouse at the moment. Last night they were talking about a young woman who used to live not far from here. It seems she was a sort of spy. She worked for a German called Brunner. I actually met this Brunner once. A repulsive man, obsessed with what he calls the Jewish problem. A couple of thugs picked this woman up yesterday afternoon. Our thugs, that is, not theirs. They made her tell them things. I don't want to talk about that, it's shameful enough having to think about it. In the end she told them about an English agent they were going to arrest. The milice, that is. Now I think perhaps she was talking about you. Do you call yourself an agent? It sounds preposterous. She said she knew where this person was to be arrested."

"Where did she say?"

"The rue Saint André des Arts, I think. Do you know that? Near the Odéon. Not a very nice area."

"Oh, yes, I know it. Did she say when?"

"She thought it must have already happened. I don't think she knew much about it."

"Where is she now, this woman? Can I see her? Where are they keeping her? Do you think you could arrange for me to talk to her?"

"Where is she now? In the Seine, I imagine. They shot her." She shook her head, "No, I should stop being such a coward. The truth is, *we* shot her. We all agreed to it."

She summoned up a weary smile, staring down into her lap, tugging pointlessly at the fabric of her skirt.

"I don't know where they did it. That's what the New France has brought us to. We shoot French girls. Apparently she was quite brave when it came to it." When she looked up, her eyes were full of tears.

"God, Alexandre, you know we can't keep prisoners. She knew that. It's a matter of surviving."

"But you *have* survived. The Americans will be in here in a week or two."

"And what then? You think our German friends will simply go home? Everybody is talking of an uprising, an armed insurrection." She glanced at the pistol on the table, "I suppose I am in a position to contribute a little now."

"The Americans won't march into that. Not street fighting. They've never wanted to come to Paris. Why should they? There's a garrison but Paris is mostly for old soldiers and wounded kids. All the Americans want is an orderly German retreat. They'll let them get out."

"How long have you been in Paris, Alexandre?" Not waiting for a reply, a strange ironic expression on her face, almost taunting him. "You seem very confident. Did you cross a bridge coming here? You must have …"

"It was getting dark."

"Not too dark to see the explosives. They are intended to be seen. At The Hotel de Ville as well … all the monuments ... explosives everywhere."

She crushed her cigarette into the ash tray. "And the galleries, of course. All of them. You forget what I do for a living."

"No, I don't forget. You collect pictures."

What was he to say? That her apartment was filled with imperishable masterpieces strung up on sagging cords like so many bits of junk?

"You must know I saw those folders. It's stolen stuff, isn't it? Lists of looted stuff. And it's here. Are you surprised I was sick?"

She looked away, sudden patches of red appearing high on her cheeks, her voice cutting through him.

"No, you were not sick because of folders. You are being absurd. You were sick because you were ill, or frightened ... or deceiving yourself."

"Those names? Bassano, Lévitan ... I forget the other."

"The other is Austerlitz. They mean nothing to you?" She was staring at him, "It is hard to believe. No, I see you don't."

"It's the paintings that need an explanation, not the names."

She stood up, smoothing her skirt, making for the door, changing her mind.

"So you want to know about pictures?" Holding on to the door handle, staring at him, a kind of dismissive scorn in her voice. She was very angry.

"Second tier stuff, in the main. Mostly from private collections, if you must know. You are quick to pose your questions. You think you can come here quizzing me? I'm not answerable to you. And since we come to it, you have not asked about the Renoir. Perhaps you remember?"

"The painting that fell on me?"

"You put your head through the glass. It's perhaps lucky for you I dislike that painting. Life's not like that – he should have known better."

"*Second tier stuff*, I suppose?"

She flinched at the sneer in his voice, standing looking through the window.

Alex pushed himself up in the bed, "I walked through the Marais last night. Whole streets deserted, houses emptied out, ravaged. You surely know somebody owns those paintings, even if they were abandoned."

"*Abandoned?*"

She was staring at him, shaking her head, filling the silence with an exasperated sigh.

"Listen to me, Alexandre, I'll explain something. God alone knows why I should. Perhaps for the satisfaction of hearing what you have to say when I finish. You know nothing at all. Perhaps you are to be forgiven for that, but you'd better listen. Too many people hide behind ignorance."

She was standing over him, restlessly wringing her hands, her pale face immobile. There was a horrible kind of suppressed tension about her. He might have not been there: she seemed to be explaining something to herself.

"When German troops arrived in Paris - I'm talking about the armistice - it seemed like a gift from God. We were not going to be caught up in another war. You can't believe the relief. Alright, we were to be saddled with the old fool Petain, but why not? There were worse options. And he had purchased us a sort of life. The war was lost, anyway." Her laugh was little more than a sharp intake of breath. "Give the English a kicking while we're at it, that's what we thought. A kicking for being *têtu*, you know, wooden-headed."

She held on to a strange grave smile, no longer hostile, drawing him in. "And that's how it was at first. The Germans wanted the old Paris, the one in the books. They wanted their sex French, if you like. We began inventing a past for them to live in. We joined them there. Not such a bad thing."

"Apart from the Jews, the round-ups, the arrests. Apart from slaughter camps ..."

"You are running ahead, I'm coming there. A German officer came to the gallery one day. Only one leg. All dressed up for the visit, rather charming, you'd think he'd come courting. You know what he'd brought? A Fragonard. He'd got it under his arm, wrapped up in brown paper. A landscape. An early thing, really lovely. He wondered whether it was worth anything. What could I say? I told him he was unlikely to meet anybody with enough money to buy it from him. But that was just the start. Soldiers started turning up more or less every day with things, asking for valuations, always valuations. It's embarrassing having to explain the facts of life to your new masters ..."

"Facts of life?"

"If somebody arrives with a painting and no provenance, what's the first question you must ask?"

Alex hesitated. "I suppose you ask how they came by it."

"Exact. But since I could not safely ask that question, the best I could say was that things are often copied. And that's true - I can speak with authority on the subject, it is my profession. Take that Renoir you damaged. It was stolen from the family who actually commissioned it. It's a copy."

"Thank God for that."

"I mean a copy made by Renoir. He was always copying his own work. When the owner was arrested the painting was confiscated. Is *confiscated* a better word than stolen?"

"Arrested by the Germans, you mean?"

"I think so. But we soon learned to do our own arresting."

"The paintings are the spoils of war. Is that what you're saying? And that makes it legitimate?"

"Makes what legitimate? We are not at war, Alexandre. How can there be spoils when there is no war? I know for you English war is about battles, but Paris is not London, Warsaw – places like that. War has passed us by. How do you think that miracle came about?"

Alex looked down, embarrassed.

"You have nothing to say? That Renoir? The one you butted. You saw the little plaque on it?"

"The word, *Bassano*."

"Yes. And you really don't know what that means?" She was staring intently at him, watching his face, finally turning away to light a cigarette, pulling hard on it, muttering, "He knows nothing at all. It's hopeless."

"I'm not sure what I'm supposed to know. You mean the rue de Bassano? I know that's not far from here."

"Not far at all. The painting that came into contact with your head came from a house on the corner of the rue Georges Bizet. A fabulous place. A kind of palace. At the end of the last century the family commissioned Renoir to paint all three of their little girls. One of them was arrested not long ago. She was an old woman, of course."

"What on earth for?"

"Alright, not arrested. *Interned,* if the word consoles you."

"You mean because she's Jewish?"

"Jewish, yes. Although in her case, perhaps not sufficiently French would be better. When I was told they'd taken her away, I remember thinking, being painted by Renoir would protect her, give her some kind of immunity. Like being touched by God."

"She'll be released soon enough. I don't think the Americans will wear arbitrary arrest."

Alex became conscious of the expression fixing him: a sort of exasperated reproach. He looked away.

"You think that, do you? I'm afraid release doesn't come into it. I know where they took her, you see. Too late for release, Americans or not. Well … release … it's a word you hear."

She sat in the chair at his bedside, pulling it close, the gesture a kind of conciliation.

"You don't know what I'm talking about, do you? I'm very sorry … no point being angry with you." Tears welled up, filling her eyes. "We're lost, Alexandre, don't you see? All of us. Living one sort of lie or another. And you talk about *release* …"

"But your paintings - I still don't understand …"

"They're not *my* paintings, for God's sake! Do you think I want to have anything to do with the damned things?" Her voice was choking, "Do you really think that?" She pulled a tiny handkerchief from her sleeve, holding it hard against her mouth, finally pulling it away, her eyes blazing.

94

"They bring them here. Twenty or thirty at a time … more sometimes. Forgeries, most of them. Nearly all of them. That's what I have to decide. I have no choice. A man comes every two weeks. A German, but not a soldier, he knows too much about art. He brings new paintings and takes the others away. These last few weeks he's started bringing work from banned artists. They are too easily copied, most of them … it is impossible. If I am wrong, I will be relieved of the task. Do you understand what that means?"

Seeing the tears on her cheeks, Alex could think of nothing to say. He shook his head.

"I will be arrested. There are camps. I'll be sent to one of them."

For a moment he thought she had finished. He watched her making for the door, mumbling to herself, "What's the point? He knows nothing."

"But I do know …" willing her to turn round, "everyone knows. The death camps, hellish places in Poland, dozens of them. Of course I know. But …"

She turned at last, standing in the doorway, "As you say, death camps. But no, not Poland. We have our own. That's what you don't know. We have our own. Right here in Paris."

She had gone, quietly closing the door before he had time to reply.

# twelve

THERE was no one in the kitchen when he went looking for coffee. The pot on the stove was still warm. He poured himself a cup and walked with it into the salon.

The long doors onto the balcony were wide open, Madeleine sitting in her chair, her head lolled uncomfortably against the metal rail.

She started awake as he stepped out, fearful eyes opening full on his own, recognition arriving slowly.

"Ah, so it's you, Alexandre. The bath. Did you find the towels? I was asleep. I often sleep out here. Paris is agreeably quiet these days. Can you give me a cigarette? Your neck … you cut your neck?"

He opened his case, holding it out to her. "The neck's alright, nothing serious. I've come to apologise. To say sorry."

"I was overwrought. Perhaps we both were. It's in the air at the moment, I'm used to it. You know, when you were a child you were always saying sorry. It's an English habit. Irritating."

"But I mean it … I want to explain."

"Oh, of course you mean it, that's what is irritating. Explain about what? Your doctor what's-his-name? Or your woman? Come and tell me about her. Sit here."

"They come to the same thing. I think about Justine all the time. I'd like to tell you about ..."

"No, I've changed my mind. We'll talk about her over dinner. I like talking about love when I'm eating. Stephanie made us something. Not much, I must say, but I'll find something good to drink. It's curious, I don't recall you having a girl when you were at school. Were you old enough for all that tiresome stuff? You were always here, but you never talked about a girl."

"No girl. I used to adore from a distance, that's as far as I got." He lit her cigarette, barely seeing her, his head filled with thoughts of Justine. "I remember how this place smelled. It's still the same, it smells of pictures. You know that smell, a bit like fresh putty? It used to scare me. It was not properly *domestic* somehow. It came back to me when you left me here last night. Standing in the hall ... it was as if somehow I was a boy again."

"Is this part of your apology? The scent of paint?"

"You're laughing at me. No, but I remember the pictures. They were all so raw - you know, they looked barely finished."

"In those days some of them weren't finished, so you're correct."

She was laughing, leaning her head back, squinting at him through half closed eyes, "Times change, you know."

"I suppose I thought proper pictures should be behind glass."

"Ah, I thought that was where you were going. You're leading me back to Renoir. I must say you are quite adept, Alexandre. Must we go through all that again? I am rather tired."

"I'm sorry, I suppose I was trying to be clever. It's what I do, if you want to know. My job, if you can call it a job. Teaching tricks like that. Interrogation tricks. And no, I'm not adept at all. I'm sorry."

She frowned at the word, crushing her cigarette into the saucer of her cup. Alex leaned across the table, trying to catch her eyes.

"What did you mean when you said there were camps? Camps in Paris?"

"Fetch me a drink, would you. Dubonnet. Put some gin in it if there's any there."

As he mixed the drink, she called through to him. "Pour something for yourself. That's not a man's drink."

When he came back onto the balcony she was sitting upright, her arms folded.

"That cushion. Behind my back. Now sit there while I think." She sat, fingers drumming the table, looking past him across the rooftops.

"I have to think where to start. Claude Pasquier, my framer? Why not there? You remember him? Or perhaps you don't?"

"In the gallery. I'd forgotten his name. An old chap with a leather apron. That one?"

"He wasn't so old, Alexendre. Not that much older than you. He started with me as an apprentice. You remember the shop in the Marais? Next to the clock-menders. If you could see that street now …"

"The rue Gravilliers? But I have seen it - I was there yesterday. I'd better not say what took me. It was deserted. As if some kind of plague had hit it. And these weird notices everywhere … stuck on the doors."

"All that started over a year ago." She hesitated, eyeing her cigarette, frowning at a lipstick stain, an odd cautious expression on her face. "I ask myself, am I wasting my breath? How much does little Alexandre really know? I thought *agents* were informed. I would not like it if you were pretending to know less than you do."

"I know about the Jewish Laws. It's common knowledge. And the roundups, of course. But I'd not imagined what I saw in the rue Gravilliers."

"I can't remember when exactly they took Claude. Time stops in a war – did you know that? It must be months ago. He's Jewish, of course. They took both of them on that account. You remember Sophie?" She was searching his face, waiting for him to speak, "Sophie, his wife?"

"*They* took them? You mean the Germans?"

"It was not always Germans. I think you know the man who took Claude. He was only a boy then, of course. You used to play with him. Veronique's son, I forget his name. A fat little boy, you remember?"

"Vaguely. He was called Camille. We used to rag him about his name, say he was really a girl, that sort of thing. Boys are cruel little devils. I went to the swimming baths with him once or twice. He was too fat. What about him?"

She reached down for her bag, placing it on the table, rummaging inside, pulling out his pistol. As he went to take it, she let it slip back inside.

"He fancies himself with one of those now. And you're right – he is cruel. He joined the milice. He was in the group that arrested Claude. Him and a couple of thugs. He came here the day afterwards."

"You mean to this apartment?"

"On his own. A private visit. Banging on the door like a maniac. Shouldering his way past me as if he owned the place, asking for my papers."

"You mean your *Carte*? What business is it of his?"

"He made it his business – and no, I don't mean my Carte. And why are you suddenly being so polite? You're thinking, *Why didn't she help Claude? Why did she let them take him away?* They are good questions. Why did I let a grubby gang of thugs do what they liked with my old friends?"

"I have no right to ask that question."

"God, you English. And you wonder why people hate you. Don't you realise how superior that sounds? You're so damned certain about everything. Well, I'll answer you anyway. I looked the other way. Do you think I'm proud of it? I knew what would happen to Claude and Sophie - and I looked the other way. The strange thing is, when those Jewish Laws came in, nobody thought much about it. You don't really believe things like that. Not even the church … well, they went on a bit about compulsory divorce, but even that seemed a bit rarefied. The truth is we didn't believe any of it. Not much of a defence, is it? We sold our souls for a chance of survival. I'm not sure *survival* means much if you're dead already."

"But we have it in England - it's the same everywhere. When war comes you're bound to ask about allegiances. Italians, Germans even. What do you do with them? Internment seems like rough justice, but when you're at war ... in any case, they weren't all French. Some are bound to be interned, deported even ..."

"Is that what you think? Where do you deport people to in the middle of someone else's war? Let me finish about Sophie. In the first place, she's no more Jewish than I am. In fact, I'm more Jewish. My fool of a grandfather used to boast he was half Jewish ... we were always telling him to shut up about it. No, Sophie comes from Perpignan. She has what they call a Catalan nose."

She stood up, leaning over the rail, watching a rare car creep down the street, belching black fumes. She did not turn round. He could barely hear her. "The milice. These fat schoolboys with guns. They go by how you look now. You are arrested for looking Jewish."

She turned aside, her profile stark against the egg-shell blue of the sky, one hand poised over the rail, not quite touching it, the pose an exaggerated caricature of some painting he failed to recognise.

"Do I look Jewish, would you say? What do you think of my nose, Alexandre? Should I die for my nose?"

"Aunt Madeleine, please. I'm sorry ... no, I shouldn't say that. You don't have to tell me this. Nobody owes these butchers guilt. Monsters like that always claim others are responsible. God knows, I've met enough of them."

She leaned back, drawing on her cigarette, her expression closed in on itself, impossible to decipher. "I remember they let her telephone here," her voice flat, dissembling calm. She had told this story before.

"Of course they let her use the telephone. It was a way of getting my address, adding me to one of their damnable lists. That's how little Camille knew where to come. Sophie kept shouting down the telephone, *tell them I'm not, Madame. Speak to them. Tell them I'm not.* Over and over again. It broke my heart. I could hear them banging about in the apartment. You could hear china breaking on the floor, glass as well - it's dreadful to hear things like that. But nobody came to the telephone. And she's not Jewish, that's for sure. She'd even got one of those ridiculous certificates saying she wasn't, poor woman."

Seeing the question in Alex's eyes, she hesitated, wondering how best to put something, "Living in the Jewish Quarter like that. She thought it was best. But those certificates are a hopeless charade. The first thing they ask is why you think you need one. Then they tell you it's a forgery. And the truth is most of them are. Sophie left the receiver on the table. I could hear everything. You never imagine things could come to this, do you? Not in Paris. She was crying as they dragged her away. Not shouting, just crying. Like a little girl calling for her mother. I don't think I'll ever forget that."

"Where did they take her?"

"Drancy, of course. Where else?"

"The housing estate?"

"Nobody would want to live there now. It's a kind of holding centre ... a transit camp. You know what *transit* means? They picked up all their neighbours the same day, most of that bottom end of the street. Sophie should have known the risk, living there. The watchmaker next door, he was as Jewish as they come. That was when they started rounding people up by the bus load. It was a kind of obsession. The milice would arrest you then seal your house up, until they came back for the furniture."

"*Furniture?* What about the furniture?"

"I can see you're new to Paris. It is another of the things we have learned not to see. Removal vans everywhere: hundreds of them. And we never see them."

"I saw one on the way here. I thought somebody was moving house."

101

"Paris is full of Germans, there are Americans at the gates, the English are dropping their damned bombs everywhere. And you think people choose such a time to move house?"

"I didn't think ..."

"Two days after they arrested Claude and Sophie, they came back to the gallery and made an inventory. They must have got the keys off Sophie, she always locked up. I was there that day. It was a removal company. Just two men and the municipal police. It's all legal. I suppose you can say legal. They had a paper from the Prefecture. They cleared the shop out, packed everything up. Much of what they took was mine, but when I asked they told me to take it up with the Prefecture. They wanted me out of the way. I imagine they helped themselves to a few things. Hard not to, I suppose. That's how you end up with a Fragonard under your arm."

"But you can't just turn up and steal things ..."

"Can't you, Alexandre? And who is going to stop you? Think about it. If all these Jews are to vanish, it's only right their things should vanish with them. Food, for example. Best eaten up, wouldn't you say? Before it goes off ..."

Alex went to take her hand, willing the anger from her. She pulled away.

"They cleared the shop out. Took all the stuff Claude was framing for me."

"But took it where? There are hundreds of houses in the rue Gravilliers. All this stuff?"

"Yes, it's the right question. The answer will surprise you. When they'd cleared the gallery they went up to the apartment upstairs. Their little flat. I went and looked. Everything had gone. Sophie's clothes ... all her little things ... even her underwear. The lino off the boards. Looking round I realised why. You know how places look when they are stripped like that? Sad little vacant spaces. Hardly worth the effort to have made a life there. They become nothing places. Easy to believe nobody was ever there."

"You were going to say about the furniture."

"It goes to Germany. It's packed and sent to Germany as a kind of insane recompense. It gets sent to the bombed cities. Hamburg, Munich, places like that. To replace what was lost in the raids. Not just furniture. Clothing, toys, books, everything. When it started it was on the wireless. They said it was only fair ... a just reckoning."

"Except it's stolen, all of it."

"There are laws about that now. If you don't have the right to own something, it can't be stolen, can it? That's how they think about it. It's an enormous undertaking. Dozens of trainloads a week, mostly from the station at Austerlitz."

"Surely there are protests, resistance? It's not too hard to disrupt operations like that. I used to plan ..."

"*Disrupt*? Oh, no, I thought you understood. There's something far more effective than disruption. We don't notice. Like the removal vans: it's going on all the time, but we don't notice. It was difficult at first, almost impossible, but you soon get into the way of it. It's such a small price to pay, you see. That's how they were able to set the camps up. *Concentration camps.* Slave labour to pack the goods. They send people from Drancy. The ones they're keeping back. Not shipping off straight away. But the camps are not in far-off Poland. They're right here in Paris."

"*Concentration camps*? But that's impossible ... what I mean is ... how long ...?"

"Oh, a long time. And it's perfectly possible. You see, if you look the other way, you soon believe there is nothing to see."

She reached across, patting his hand as if he had denied something. "There must be hundreds of people working in those places. God knows where they sleep. Or where they eat. Or what they eat, for that matter - they must be fed somehow. Or perhaps not. There you are - it's best not to ask."

"So you have all these people in prisons ..."

"You can't pack furniture in a prison. No, you've seen where they are. Those labels you were so interested in."

"Bassano?"

"They send the best stuff there. Fine antiques, the best of the paintings, things that need specialists to repair. Specialist prisoners, that is. I think there's a special place they send pianos. You can't imagine how many pianos are being transported every day around Paris while your war is going on. And linen – bales and bales of linen – I believe they pack linen at the Lévitan store. Not that anyone knows, of course."

"You mean the furniture shop? I remember that place. Cheap stuff. It was a sort of Woolworths."

"Not at all. The place is closed, of course, but it's not so cheap now. If you could shop there … you'd find it had gone up in the world."

# thirteen

THEY sat late into the night in a tiny island of candlelight on the balcony, drinking Chambolle-Musigny, picking at the salad Stephanie had set out for them, the city beyond a vast mosaic of flickering yellow pinpricks. Warm air rising from the quiet street filled Alex with an almost unbearable nostalgia, the scent of an unrecoverable time before the blight of war.

"This woman you say you were looking for." She was leaning forward, resting on one elbow, waiting for Alex to light her cigarette.

"She is English, after all? Does she have a family?"

"Her mother died when she was very young. She's half French, I think. Brought up by nuns. Somewhere in the South West."

"Nuns. My God. Poor soul!"

"Oh, I don't know. She said she was happy enough. She kept her faith, anyway ..."

"And you say ended up a spy. No, Alexandre, don't look at me like that. You can keep your faith out of revenge. There are nuns and nuns, believe me. What makes you so sure she's in Paris?"

"They told her I had been posted here. Probably said I was in danger. That would be enough for her to try and follow me. All lies, of course."

"Now you're being mysterious. You make her sound very naïve, to come running after you. Why should she do that?"

"I don't know. Don't you understand? I don't know. In my job when things seem obvious, you get suspicious. Justine killed someone in France. A German officer. They don't forget things like that."

"This *they* you continually mention?"

The sardonic look over the rim of her glass said she did not expect a reply. She stared into the dark, her cigarette a tiny red dot between her fingers. The lights of a solitary car below threw long shadows across the front of the buildings opposite. She stood up, pushing her chair back.

"I remember you in this mulish mood. I see you're not going to explain." She glanced at her watch, "That girl is late again. It's getting damp. Shall we go in?"

Alex did not move, looking down at the tiled floor. "He would have been born in October. I always think of him as *he*. I have dreams about him, you know?"

"Does that sort of talk comfort you?" Standing behind him she rested one hand briefly on his shoulder. "I understand more than you think, you know. Your Justine cannot be here, that much is obvious. Not with a child – it's impossible. A romantic fiction. Who would send a pregnant woman …?"

"Who's talking about *send*? Perhaps she had no choice."

"Shall we go inside? There is coffee."

Alex craned round, looking over his shoulder. "*Girl with Straw Hat*. You know a painting with that title?"

"You mean the Bradley painting? Of course. I actually saw it last year. He showed it in the *Salon d'Automne*."

"No, not that. There's a painting of Justine with that title. By an artist called Lucile Beyrou."

Madeleine frowned, shaking her head, "Beyrou? No, the name means nothing."

"You won't know her by that name."

"And the title is in English, like the Bradley?"

"No, French - *Fille au Chapeau de Paille*."

"Not particularly good French, I must say. You can see why Bradley stuck to English."

She stepped inside the salon, calling back to him, her voice suddenly impatient, "There must be thousands of such paintings, Alexandre. French girls in straw hats. Renoir did his fair share. He was always painting them - regrettable things, but certainly full of hats. Why are you asking this?"

Alex followed her inside, standing awkwardly, waiting until she flopped onto the sofa, waving him into a seat opposite.

"She adopted this Beyrou name when we got her out. We set her up in Dundee. In Scotland. She had worked with Bradley in France for years. She was almost as famous as him. Lived at his house in the South West."

"Ah, you mean that English girl ... I forget her name. There was an exhibition just before the war. Yes, her work was excellent. I heard she had been magically spirited away. So that was where you put her – Scotland."

"I wasn't involved, but Justine was one of the agents who did the spiriting. I think that's why she tracked her down. She actually lived with her in Dundee for a few weeks."

"And it was this so-called Beyrou who painted her?"

"She said she did it as a kind of a consolation."

"Ah, I see. But you say your Justine is – how do you put it? A secret agent, a spy?"

"She was an agent."

"But a portrait? Would that not be incredibly unwise? For the artist as well."

"Perhaps. But it was something private, between them. By some hellish mischance it ended up on display. Someone bought it."

"So ...? You are being mysterious again."

"I told you I came to Paris to look for a man. In the world in which I work I count him as dangerous. I believe he bought the painting. He recognised Justine."

"And wants to avoid others doing the same – is that what you're saying?"

"Or to expose her. Either seems possible. He may have brought the painting with him to Paris. That's the rock I am clinging to. It must mean Justine is still alive."

"And your child?" Her eyes suddenly searching, "If it is your child? Is that your concern? Is it? This word, *consolation*. She is in need of consolation?"

Seeing the pain in his face, she slowly shook her head. "It's hard to believe in this rock you cling to. The man who deals with the collection at the Bassano house is very knowledgeable. He is coming here tomorrow to collect paintings. I will see what I can prise out of him."

"He's coming here?"

"In the morning. You cannot be here. He tends to wander about. Go and look at Paris for a few hours. Sit in a café somewhere. It is safe enough. Or go for a walk. Not too far. You may see some bread."

"But it's rationed."

"Ah, but the strangest people sell bread. You imagine Paris can manage without bread? You have money I assume? Ask in a café ... if it looks safe."

"Is it safe to look at this Bassano prison? It can't be far to walk. There are people in London who would like to know about what's going on there. Is it safe?"

"No, it's not far. But there is nothing to see at Bassano. And it's not a prison. All you will see is a huge town house. God knows how many are locked inside, but you will see nobody. And no, it is not safe. The street is too quiet. The furniture deliveries are mostly at the Lévitan Store. You might see something there but it's much too far to walk. Near the Gare du Nord."

"I don't mind walking. A railway station gives the perfect reason to be there. But if I'm stopped ... I don't trust my papers."

"Oh, you wouldn't be stopped. Not any longer. We used to be harassed all the time - police, Gendarmes, even German soldiers if they liked the look of you. Then a few months ago all that nonsense petered out. It's as if they've lost interest. More likely, they think it's no longer wise to take sides. Of course, you have the milice to worry about, but it's Jews they're after. Just try not to look like a Jew, my dear." She choked back a laugh, her face defiantly pink. "No, I agree. A joke in bad taste. Your disapproval is noted."

"What right have I to disapprove? I've not lived through all that. I can't imagine ..."

"Can't imagine what keeps us amused in this madhouse? Is that what you meant? You'd be surprised. Sometimes it's best to laugh."

She stood up, pulling him to stand in front of her, placing two hands on his shoulders, straightening him as if he were setting out for school.

"You'd pass. You look too respectable to arrest. Just one thing – you will need a respectable hat to go out in. I will find one for you tomorrow. I have quite a collection of abandoned hats. And something for your neck, the neck spoils the impression."

She handed him a tiny visiting card. "Give them this address if you are very unlucky."

She was already at the door. "Your gun will remain here. That way you can't shoot anybody. Now I think I'll go to bed."


One side of the Faubourg Saint-Martin was filled with the early morning crowd streaming down from the Gare du Nord, past the stone facade of the Lévitan Store. Dusty plate glass windows streaked with bird droppings gave the place an unkempt air, somewhere that had known better days. Plainly it had been closed for months.

Two soldiers stood between fake marble pillars, their backs against the locked doors, watching the crowd. Shabby uniforms, khaki and green, flashes of red high on the sleeve. It gave them a vaguely Russian air.

Alex fell in behind a press of women with prams, stopping as they stopped, turning side-on to gawp through the grimy windows.

Inside, crude makeshift screens a few feet high set off tiny display areas, each with its collection of sofas, chairs, tables, beds – sad little caricatures of pre-war domesticity. Decorative lamps on tall stands, their shades no longer straight, were lined up along the back wall.

A removal van, braking hard, buried itself too fast down the steep ramp between two narrow arches, the woman in front jerking her pram up onto the pavement, jostling into him, bellowing curses down the cavernous space.

The soldiers in the doorway came nervously down the steps to look, holding their line as prams pushed towards them. One of them nervously unhitched his rifle.

Alex wandered a few yards down the vacant ramp.

In the half light at the bottom, men were already swinging open the back doors of the van. It was stuffed with furniture, wrapped in grey blankets, spindly kitchen chairs roped together, leaning out.

A silent line of anonymous figures dressed in long striped aprons had already begun to unload, pulling out tea chests and cardboard boxes, mechanically passing them along to disappear through a doorway at the side.

The driver stood aimlessly leaning against the side of the van. He flicked a cigarette into the yard, gesturing to Alex to move away.


At the top of the ramp the squabble had ended. The woman with the pram was walking slowly up the road towards the station.

The guards were back against the huge glass doors.

Uncertain for a second which way to go, Alex stepped out of the darkness onto the pavement, flinching back as something dark angled through his vision, momentarily blotting out the sun.

A massive swish of air scythed past his face, some gigantic bird swooping on him, talons extended like thin gyrating legs.

A sack of something soft thumped onto the pavement in front of him, a single sickening bounce bursting bits of coloured cloth out into the gutter.

It was over before he had time to move, before he had time to see. A mound of rags lay pressed against the pavement, red and black, pierced here and there with tiny beads. As he watched, a single naked arm flopped out, white flesh spattered to the wrist with blood.

The soldiers were already barging him aside, reaching down to the body, crumpled uniforms caked in grime, muttering in a language he had never heard before, their yellow complexion more Mongolian than German.

They pulled a piece of the cloth aside, bending down to look. Part of an innocent pretty face was watching them from under a halo of light brown hair. She could not have been more than twenty, little more than a girl. And frail. You would have thought too frail to fall so fast.

A crowd had formed behind, hemming him in, someone calling, *Cover the poor soul up.*

A man at Alex's side muttered, *I saw the whole thing. She jumped I tell you. Is it a woman?*

Blood had begun to seep from the bundle, a magenta stain spreading out from the woman's head.

One of the soldiers grabbed Alex's arm, steadying himself, scraping at a fold in her dress with his foot to cover her face. He would not look down.

It seemed an age before a German officer appeared at the top of the ramp, pushing his way through the crowd.

Alex freed himself, drifting to the edge of the pavement, hemmed in, forced to stand and watch.

The officer muttered something that sent the guards scuttling back to their post by the door. He lit a cigarette, standing next to the body, head tipped back, staring at the row of tiny windows on the fourth level where the leaded surface of a flat roof reached out to a stretch of decorative tiles. He stood blowing smoke into the air, waiting.

An improvised stretcher appeared with two bearers, pistols tucked into their belts. They stood next to the mound of cloth, nervously looking across to the sullen crowd on the other side of the street. Perhaps the officer said something – it was impossible to hear.

Someone called, *fucking milice. Leave her alone.*

A man at Alex's side ducked down, picking a stone out of the gutter. A wave of silence swept over the crowd, a gigantic intake of breath. He threw it hard at one of the plate glass windows high on the second floor. In the frozen moment they heard the sharp clink as it bounced down to the pavement. The officer daintily kicked it away, grimacing as his shoes scraped the pavement.

As if the rattle against the unbroken glass had been some unspoken command, Alex found himself staring at a sudden line of faces at the window. Unnaturally white, like painted puppet heads, they hovered an instant then vanished, as if snatched away by hidden strings.

It could not have been more than a second, but Alex felt his world dissolve. Rooted where he stood, his head cocked absurdly back, he stared at the blank of the glass.

The heads had long since gone. Perhaps a dozen, women all of them, faces white against the darkness of the space inside, all but one with scarfs covering their hair.

Pressed in a milling crush of angry people he found he could not move, desperately clinging to the tiny fraction of time in which his eyes had locked with hers: time shared, certainty for ever sure. He stumbled forward as someone tried to drag him away, an odd surging sensation in his chest catching his breath. Standing his ground, it seemed he dare not move. Moving would shake the image away. Dark eyes, their expression fleeting desperation.

The men had reluctantly loaded the stretcher, staggering back towards the ramp. The officer walked to the edge of the pavement calling to the crowd to disperse. Someone shouted, *Move off yourself. We live here.* He unbuttoned the holster at his hip, flicking the leather flap open and closed, facing them down.

Conscious that it was in some obscure way a betrayal, Alex turned with the crowd, letting himself be swept back to the junction of the Faubourg Saint-Martin.

# fourteen

WHEN he got back, Madeleine was sitting on the balcony drinking coffee. She seemed preoccupied, barely listening as he blurted out the story in an incoherent rush of words.

She looked up, as if seeing him for the first time, blinking.

"Wait. You say you were outside the Lévitan shop? We were a little drunk last night. I hardly believed you were serious. I thought you were going to a café. You realise it's a secret place? Guarded. There's nothing to see from the outside – just an empty shop. I was there last year to collect a picture ... at least, you would think it was empty."

"You mean you went inside? I didn't know that."

"Why should you know?" snapping at him, patches of red on her cheeks, "all I remember was the smell. An overpowering smell of unclean humanity. I suppose all prisons are like that, except this place seemed deserted. I was left to wait in a big hall. They called it the lobby, divided up into little private spaces. I suppose where they met customers, when there were customers to meet. My God, you took a risk going all that way. A risk for both of us. There's nothing out of the ordinary there, apart from the disagreeable smell."

"You don't think suicide out of the ordinary?"

"No ..." She paused as if the question demanded reflection. "Not particularly. Suicide is not unusual in Paris. You could say it's an occupational hazard for some."

"Soldiers on guard duty for an empty shop - not unusual either? They were certainly not French, not German either. I think the uniform was Russian."

"Ah, our famous Uzbeks. I'm not sure what country that is. Perhaps you know? They were deserters from the Russian front. Changed sides. It shows you are new to Paris, Alexandre, you meet them everywhere. Professional thugs. The Germans use them for dirty jobs they won't do themselves."

She looked at him, shaking her head, the expression something he remembered from years ago – grudging disbelief barely disguising a faint approving smile for some act of infantile bravado.

"So little Alexandre walked on his own all that way? I begin to feel responsible for you. Perhaps you really are mad."

"What am I supposed to do? Alright, perhaps I drank a little too much. You realise you were talking about concentration camps in the centre of Paris? It may be real to you, but it was always going to seem unreal to me ... until I saw for myself. And thank God I did. If I hadn't ..."

"So you went. And it is still unreal. You see phantoms. This nonsense about faces at the window."

"I saw her, I tell you. Justine is in that place. For God's sake, why don't you accept what I say?"

"Leave God out of it, Alexandre. You saw a face, just a woman's face. For a few seconds. You say you spend your life hoping to see this woman. You told me it had made you a little mad, do you remember?"

"Not so mad that I imagine things."

"Mad enough to think you should wave pistols at me. What did you really see? A face. Tell the truth, how many times have you taken some complete stranger for your missing woman?"

"Her name is Justine. Dozens of times, I suppose. But ..."

"There you are. Perhaps we can finish with this nonsense. The truth is, you *wanted* to see her."

"I don't understand. It's as if you want me to be wrong. As if you wish it. Why won't you believe me? *Why*? I understand these things – it is my profession. If I'd made a mistake, by now I would be doubting myself, starting to feel stupid. But I don't. Not in the slightest. We were looking straight into each other's eyes. It was Justine."

"Then God help her, the poor soul!" The ferocity in her voice struck him like a blow. He stood nervously looking down at her, aware only of the quiet flap of the table-cloth in the breeze.

It was a long time before she spoke.

"I'm sorry, my dear, I didn't mean to shout. It's been a difficult day. Come and sit down, I need to talk to you. About my morning."

"Of course. I forgot. The man who came for the pictures."

"Two men this time - the usual man and someone else. I have to tell you about him. He was not in uniform, but I knew him. It was Herr Brunner himself. I told you I met him once in the Lévitan store. He's in charge of the Jewish clearances in the city. I don't think he remembered me. I can't be sure. He is truly terrifying. Eyes everywhere."

"Too many questions?"

"Only one question, but it was enough. He asked whether he could admire the view from my balcony. How could I refuse?"

She waved despairingly at the table, her hands extended. "Two coffee cups. He saw them."

She reached out resting one hand on his arm. "He said they won't be bringing pictures here any more. Some other arrangement is to be made. I had to listen to them arguing about it."

She seemed unable to go on, looking down at her lap, idly picking at a thread on her dress, mumbling to herself.

"If I had known you were going there I would have paid more attention," fumbling for a handkerchief, tears sliding softly down her cheeks. "There's no call to look like that. We all cry now. There is a lot to cry about. That's what they were discussing - the Lévitan Store. Apparently deliveries of food have stopped. Something about a strike. You understand what I'm saying? There has been no food in that place for days. Brunner was ranting that he had no interest in pictures when there were prisoners to think about. Prisoners were more important."

"What d'you mean, no food?"

"You think he cares about food?" Her voice cut through him like ice. "What sort of a man do you think this Brunner is? God almighty, do you think I wanted to listen to this hideous German going on about his starving Jews? About *his* starving Jews, that's how he put it. It made me sick. He doesn't care whether they ever eat again. All he sees is the chance to ship one more consignment of the poor devils to their death. You knew under French law the prisoners in Lévitan could not be deported?"

"I know nothing about it. Because they're not Jews?"

"There are rules. Rules of definition. I'm ashamed to talk about it. We spend our lives now debating who's a proper Jew, who's half a Jew, a quarter Jew, and so on and so on. Even wife of Jew - as if it was something you could catch like the 'flu. You can die now for some scrap of paper your mother put away in a drawer."

She had talked herself into silence, staring blankly into space, breathing hard. She seemed unaware he was still there.

"The prisoners?" Alex sat down opposite her, leaning across the little table. "You were talking about the prisoners in the Lévitan store."

"You mean your Justine?" Her tight little smile somehow set his heart thumping. "You think you really did see her? Herr Brunner has decided to tear up the rules that put her there. All the rules. I heard him say it right here. He was shouting at this other man, saying that calling people non-deportable was just a French trick. *Stringing things out* – that's how he put it. His French is very good. The orders have already been given. Half the prisoners are to be taken to Austerlitz tonight. All the young men. There is no appeal. No one to appeal to."

"The rail station?"

"They will be loaded tonight for Poland. Convoy number 77. He kept saying that number. He was proud of it. I don't know why."

"And the others? The women?"

"It's a trick. He has told the women and old men they will be released later today. He wants them out of the way while they handle the men. They've been given a *Quittance* and told to fend for themselves for food. Find food from relatives, friends, anybody. Or a church soup kitchen. All a lie, of course. They will be rounded up tomorrow. Added to the convoy."

"But you said *released*. Once she's out …"

"Wandering about with just a meaningless bit of paper. You realise you can be arrested if you have no papers, Jewish or not? It happens a lot at the train station. They take them to the goods yard. It's best to pretend you don't hear the shots. Brunner's trick means they'll arrest whoever helps as well. Whole families, men, women, children. No concessions for children, they take less space, you see. Trains loaded with children leave Paris all the time. Who's going to risk their life to help a starving Jew? Would you?"

She looked up at him, her eyes dead. "I let them take Sophie away."

"But released later today?" He had stood up, looking round, lost to a sense of weary desperation. For a while, finding Justine in that place had seemed a kind of miracle. Madeleine's face told him the truth of the matter. He tried again.

"You said later today? So there's still time. There must be. I can go back. I must go back. Keep watch somehow."

She looked away, embarrassed, easing herself out of her chair. As she walked into the salon she gave him a tiny patient smile, tugging at his sleeve to follow her.

"Wait here a moment, I have to look for something. I will not be long."

The click of her feet faded as she hurried across the hall and along the corridor. He heard the study door close.


"I have a friend with a shop near the Faubourg Saint-Denis. Not far from the Lévitan store." She had come back into the salon carrying a flat parcel tied with string.

"Her name is Beatrice Verne - that's Verne like the writer. She sells art materials. If you're stopped, you're taking this to her gallery. It's an old print for framing. The address is on the parcel. It's not much of a place ... on the corner, if I remember right."

"*Passage du Desir*." He looked up from the address on the parcel.

"Not what you think," an odd ironic snort of a laugh, "and no place for loitering. It has a reputation. Street girls use it. If she's closed ..." she shrugged, "another roll of the dice. Tell Beatrice there is a letter from me inside the parcel. It asks her to frame the print and says Alexandre is delivering it. I used to talk about you, she might remember. Ask her if you can watch the Lévitan store from her upstairs window. You won't see much, but at least you won't be outside inviting someone to arrest you. It's the best I can do. I am not rolling the dice."


The shop on the corner of the *Passage* smelled of turpentine and Madame Verne's incessant cigars. The place was cramped, just room to stand wedged against a long mahogany counter.

She took the packet from him, hearing his stammered request in silence, her back to the door, holding Madeleine's letter in two trembling hands.

She led him painfully up three arthritic flights of stairs to a storeroom, standing in the doorway as he dragged a table to the window, kneeling on it, pressing his forehead against the dusty glass.

She watched him for a while, a puzzled expression on her face, until a bell tinkled at the shop door below.

She stumped away down the wooden stairs, leaving him alone.

Madeleine had been right. Far below, a slow succession of removal vans laboured up and down the ramps. Beyond the corner of the street a sign: *AUX CLASSES LABORIEUSES* was picked out in glossy rain-washed tiles.

The morning guards still leaned against the double doors watching the vans drop out of view. An endless stream of people from the station hurried past. No one seemed interested in deliveries to a shop that had been closed for years.

Pressed against his windowpane, Alex let himself fall into a kind of sleepy catatonia, the pain in his knees retreating to no more than a tolerable obscure ache. The endless afternoon wore on, the bell in the shop below his only connection with reality.

No one left the Lévitan store.

The patch of sky to the north darkened to a deeper blue, Paris relaxing into warm twilight. It was getting late. A little while ago a brief square of yellow light had appeared high on the fourth floor of the store. Snuffed out as someone tugged a blackout curtain across.

A church clock somewhere close struck eight.

The guards suddenly stepped forward, standing to attention as a polished Mercedes staff car slid silently to a halt.

A German officer in dress uniform jumped down, standing a moment on the pavement, arching his back, peering up to the roof. The driver scuttled round to open the rear doors, two women clambering out, sweeping up the steps past the guards, laughing at the cascade of ritual salutes. They disappeared inside through the double doors.

The officer said something to the guards, turning away to light a cigarette. He stood looking down at the dark patch where the pavement had been washed.

Two delivery vans had come and gone before the women returned, setting boxes and cartons down for the driver to pack, squealing in mock protest as a package was manhandled, tugging it from him, cradling it into the car in their arms.

It was getting dark, shadows falling over the silent store.

The officer watched the car drive off, pacing the pavement, pausing to check his watch. Not long ago crowds of people had been pushing past. With the chime of the clock an odd deserted air had settled on the street.

A car drew up opposite, three men jumping out to join the officer. They stood leaning against the car, looking across to the street. Alex heard Madame Verne pulling the shutters closed, slamming the shop door, the bell jangling hysterically.

He jumped down from the table as she reached the landing outside his tiny room, wheezing heavily. She pushed past him, making for the window, peering into the street, calling over her shoulder, "There was an accident this morning. They are looking for witnesses. They will be coming here. Hurry, while they make their minds up. When you go out turn left."

"*Left?* I didn't come that way."

"They will block the Faubourg. Go down the *Passage*."

"But go where? Where does it go to?"

"Hurry Monsieur. Don't wait for me. You will arrive on the rue Lafayette. Can you find your way?"

"Yes, I think so."

"Just go straight. You will come to the church. But hurry."

"*Church?* What church?"

"That's where they go looking for their food. The people from the store. The Lévitan. No, don't you go saying anything ... you're looking for somebody, aren't you? You would have been better doing your looking at the church. I could have told you, but you said the front of the shop. They never come out there."

The whistle sounded as he reached the first bend in the narrow alleyway. A single long blast, reminding him of the raid on the rue Saint André des Arts. Hearing the sound, a man coming towards him turned abruptly, walking away fast. They arrived together at the junction of three streets, the man glancing at Alex, hesitating. He scuttled down an alley to the left, echoing footsteps cut off as he reached the turn.

Alex looked back. The length of the *Passage* as far as the first bend was still empty. The whistle had stopped. Ahead, at the far end, traffic on the rue Lafayette ran left and right.

He was on a triangular patch of land in front of a church, a plaque declaring *Eglise Saint Laurent* fixed to an iron gate closed with a rusty chain. Dead leaves and old newspapers had pressed themselves under a mossy stone bench in an elaborate carved entrance. Weeds sprouted between the flagstones. No one had passed that way for months. The place had long since been abandoned.

Further down the *Passage* a restless little queue of people had formed outside a door, the murmur of soft voices reaching where he stood. They fell silent for a man with a wicker basket walking along the line handing out what looked like bits of paper. As Alex reached them the sociable murmur of talk fell quiet, letting him shuffle by.

Seen from the junction his first wild thoughts had been of prisoners in search of food, but these were no cowed convicts. They were mostly women, dressed as if for some event.

One, taller than the rest, turned towards him as he walked past, a sudden glimpse of dark hair setting a frantic lurch in his chest. A hard-faced woman in her summer best despatched the thought with a brief anaemic smile.

Remembering Madeleine's final words, Alex found himself absurdly scanning one mild disinterested face after another, the rising sense of anti-climax almost comic. He pushed past, thinking only that the dice had been rolled and he had lost. Whatever these well-dressed people were waiting for, it was not food. Whoever they were, Justine was not among them.

As he walked on, the memory of the faces at the window seemed to alter, taking on the quality of some dream he would never quite recall.

He glanced back hearing the slow shuffle of footsteps. They had disappeared, the swell of voices fading as the door grated over stone.

For the first time since he had arrived in Paris Alex knew in his heart that Justine was irredeemably lost.

# fifteen

A T the point where the *Passage* joined the rue Lafayette the street lights flared into life in a hiss of gas, the contrast plunging the deserted alleyway behind into darkness.

Two Gendarmes were standing on the corner, silhouetted against the stream of traffic, blocking the way for those fleeing the raid on the Faubourg Saint-Denis.

They turned into the *Passage*, walking side by side out of the light, batons swinging in amiable synchrony, talking quietly together, close enough for him to hear. Alex had nowhere to go.

He walked quickly back the way he had come, keeping close to the wall. As he came to the closed door, a faint line of yellow light sparked underneath in a burst of muffled music. Heavily carved, the door was black with years of varnish, its pointless central knob polished bright. There was no keyhole – if it was locked, it must be from inside.

The steady beat of footsteps seemed very close. There was a slight bend in the *Passage* at his back. Once past that, they must see him. He pushed at the door, feeling it yield, slipping past the open crack into a cushion of warm air.

He was inside a tiny porch, bare stone walls stained green with damp, everywhere the overpowering smell of warm church mould.

A framed portrait of the ancient Marechal hung on a nail next to Christ, both a little awry.

A line of light leaked through a division in felt-lined double doors. Beyond, a voice intoned Latin into echoing space.

The outer door had swung to, its catch resting against an iron lock. He pressed against the wall, straining to listen, the beat of his heart comingled with voices as the Gendarmes passed. They did not pause.

Alex looked at his watch. He would give them two minutes - enough to know if they were coming back – then make a run for the rue Lafayette.

He leaned against the door, breathing hard, to find it pushed in against him, throwing him off balance, an old woman stumbling inside, clutching his arm to steady herself. They stood for a second swaying together before she pulled away, still holding his arm, precipitating them through the padded doors into a fug of candle heat and dim light.

They were inside a vast cathedral space, the tiny congregation barely visible, huddled into two scant rows near the door. Startled heads craned round as the woman clattered into a pew, pushing Alex hard against a pillar, hemming him at her side.


Penned in with no escape, Alex remembered little of the service apart from the sermon. A call to arms, the priest reminding the tiny congregation how Cyril of Jerusalem sold church plate to feed starving prisoners. It was received in silence.

Alex scanned his ancient parishioners' startled backs. They seemed unlikely revolutionaries. It was hard to believe they knew many prisoners, starving or otherwise. They had probably occupied their Sunday pews for half a century.

As the Latin recommenced Alex thought of Archer's celebration, remembering *not impossible,* remembering feverish days of anticipation. Justine had not been there: she was not here either.

He heard the service out in an agony of impatience, stumbling through a half-remembered final hymn. Nobody had left the store after the two women had driven away. It would be madness to go back now. Hopes ebbed as the stained glass windows over the altar grew black. It was too late.

Alex knelt as the woman at his side creaked down, the priest rattling through a benediction.

As the congregation filed out, a man leaned over to exchange a greeting with the woman, including Alex with a perfunctory nod. They lingered on for endless seconds, finally easing out into the vacant aisle. She took the man's arm, joining a straggling queue at the door.

Now he was free to escape, awareness of the futility of his search swept over him in a seductive wave of weariness. It was at least as sensible to sit on here, lost in the drowsy scent of incense, as to pointlessly wander the streets.

He leaned back against the wooden rail of the pew, listening to the hundred tiny echoing sounds of an empty church.

At the end of the aisle, the priest had begun to snuff the candles, spirals of smoke curling up into the still air. He reached behind a pillar for some secret switch, an echoing click returning the chancel steps to darkness, shuffling on, extinguishing candles as he came.

That was when Alex saw her. Silhouetted against a yellow pattern of votive lights, pausing to adjust the scarf at her throat. She began to walk, her feet soft on the patterned tiles. He waited immobile in his station, lost to the throb of his heart. She had reached him now, walking past, dark eyes lost in some hellish misery of their own. Eyes he had searched a million times fixed ahead on nothing at all.

It seemed she might have walked on, compressed into herself, barely present, Alex willing her to turn, willing her to find him there, barely daring to break some hideous spell.

"Justine."

She turned to the whispered word, startled eyes wide alight.

A tiny escritoire served Madeleine for a dressing table. Ancient veneered wood polished to the colour of honey, the flap left pulled down to accommodate a jumble of little boxes and perfume flasks.

A porcelain ring-stand, empty, kept a stack of opened letters at bay.

Far into the night Alex kept vigil at Justine's side, comforted by restless movements borne to his chair pressed hard against her bed.

Settling her to sleep they had found a folded sheet of paper clutched tight in her right hand. A kind of crude *Quittance*, the names filled in on a dotted line, thanking Madame Isobel Fortieu, spouse of Corporal Thierry Fortieu, for service to the Republic, releasing her *Sine Die* from further service in the Lévitan store. An illegible signature appeared over yesterday's date.

She had pulled the sheets high against her chin, fists clenched against the cloth, tiny spasms of distress battling sleep. A bruise on one cheek spread towards her ear like a smudge of purple paint. A tic at the edge of her mouth endlessly wrinkled her eyes with pain.

Hours earlier, Madeleine had brought him soup, bending over, calmly examining the sleeping form.

"She will not wake tonight."

She straightened up easing the stiffness from her back. "You too. You should sleep. I'll hear her if she wakes up."

Alex shook his head, the first true smile for many days. "When she wakes she won't know where she is. I'm better here."

She continued looking down at the bed, the expression on her face something he had never seen before.

"So this is your Justine. She looks very young. Like a child. She is very thin. Strange to see little Alexandre's woman. I confess I never quite believed in her. All the same ..." her smile was frank, "I ask myself whether this madman with a pistol deserves his sleeping princess. She looks, how shall I say it? Wholesome. Perhaps that's not the right word."

"Yes, it's the right word. And no, I don't deserve her. I never can."

She walked to the window, checking the curtains, the faint sound, *tch, tch*, his disapproving aunt of years ago.

"No, Alexandre, you can't say that. She owes you her life. You must let her thank you for that. You are not heroic enough to be so modest. Now, I am going to find somewhere to sleep. It will be morning soon. Don't forget to eat your soup. The bread was fresh. Can you believe it? Impossible to find fresh bread in Paris."

She left the door ajar, an angled finger of yellow light reaching out to touch the edge of the sheet.


The sound of a rifle shot jolted him awake. A single shot so painfully close he thought at first it had been in the room. Hauled out of muddled sleep, finding nothing familiar, conscious only of the violent echo in his head.

He fumbled at something slipping from his lap.

He had been walking the empty corridors of Torridon in a dream of confused twilight, sporadic gunfire from the snowbound hills. Checking room after empty room, searching for students, fretting he had forgotten what he must tell them. He woke with the guilty thought it was better they should never know.

Justine was sitting up in bed, smiling into his eyes.

"I'm afraid I ate your soup. My need was greater."

She raised one hand to cover the bruise on her cheek, her expression almost embarrassed, oddly vulnerable.

"God Alex, don't look so hard, you'll burn me." She stretched out a hand to him. "Good morning, Guffin … damnation, I knew saying that would set me off again. I've been sitting here weeping. It was lovely."

"How long have you been awake? I'm sorry, I was so sure I would never fall asleep. God, Madeleine? Have you …?"

"Been and gone long ago. Kissed me, said good morning, said she's your aunt, then said she was off in search of a ration of bread. If she's your aunt, Alex, that's good enough for me. I never knew you

128

had an aunt. I must say she smells delicious. Apparently I'm in her bed."

She wriggled down until only her head was visible.

"I've been looking at my Alex. I think you were dreaming. Not about me, I hope. You seemed in a state. That blanket you pushed off was Madeleine's idea. She said you looked cold. Now, I'm tired of talking. I want to go back to sleep. Just for a while, my love. You can leave me ... I feel perfectly safe. There's so much to tell you. But sleep first. I'm dreadfully tired."

Alex got up, awkwardly freeing the stiffness from his body.

"I'm not far away. I'll hear if you call."

As he reached the door she called to him, her remembered voice bringing tears to his eyes. "I did see you, you know. When was it? At the window. It's been a kind of miracle, hasn't it?"

Caught in the doorway, looking back, he found he could not reply. She was already asleep, a gaunt face white against the cover. She seemed calmer, her mouth settled into something like a smile.


Madeleine was in the kitchen making coffee in a saucepan. She put a finger to her lips, pushing the door closed behind him, whispering.

"Stephanie takes Monday off. She has this diabolical thing she calls her Moka pot. I won't touch it. A saucepan will do for us. There were eggs at the bakers if you want to risk them. I can make an omelette." She glanced at the door, "Still asleep I suppose? Last night was like something from an opera. She seemed barely alive."

"Walking all that way, it nearly put paid to her. She's dreadfully weak. I thought I would have to carry her, but she held on, thank God. She kept saying the metro was too much of a risk. And she was right, there was a little band of thugs with pistols checking papers outside the Miromesnil metro. Your milice chaps, I think. I saw them eying Justine but we walked past arm in arm. They were almost as nervous as us. They're not getting things their own way so much, people were arguing, telling them to stop pestering. They didn't stop us. It was single men they were looking for I suppose. We passed for a couple."

"But you *are* a couple, my dear. I've seen that for myself. And don't ever call those milice bastards mine. Did you hear the shot this morning? I was coming back with the bread. One of them was trying to get his motorcycle going. Somebody took a shot at him from an upstairs window. He took off like a frightened girl, pushing the thing along the road. Not too dignified. People in the bakers were saying the Americans will be here in a day or two. You must have seen the posters all over the place. *Victory is Near.* All of a sudden we're fighting a war. Victory – I ask you? You can't help thinking it's a bit late to be brave. God knows what's to become of us. Nothing's changed – the place is still full of Germans."

She came closer, suddenly serious, whispering. "I was thinking how we get her away. She is in dreadful danger. She'll need papers. You as well, if you are to be a couple. That will be harder. How much does she know?"

"I don't know. She thinks she's safe."

"And she is, for now. But I can't help wondering when Herr Brunner will remember that second coffee cup."

## sixteen

HE spent the rest of that day sitting alone on the little balcony, looking out across a patchwork of leaded rooftops wavering in the rising heat, the distant horizon curving slightly under an unflinching brazen sky.

He was possessed by a sense of waiting for something undefined, perhaps something he had forgotten, filling him with a restless vague anxiety. The street below seemed complicit: holding its breath, silent but for occasional furtive footsteps.

Justine came to the doorway behind him as the mantle clock in the salon chimed five. Barefoot, her hair still wet from the bath, wearing a patterned robe, a little too short. She stood poised on the threshold, breathing in the air.

Easing himself out of the chair Alex found himself closer than he expected, turning aside, embarrassed.

She took both his hands in hers. "Yes, I know. Odd isn't it? It's like we've just met. I feel new-born somehow. Very queer. As if I didn't know my dear old Guffin. Stay there, let me look at you. And it's the truth, you do look a bit different. Me as well. Of course I do, I see it in your face. Best not to look … not just yet. Come inside and sit with a friendly ghost."

Lost for where to start, he looked beyond her into the salon.

"Madeleine?"

"She said she had to go out. That's twice. I think she's being discreet. Very French. She's going to cook us something when she gets back. She says she barely remembers how, so we shall have to suffer. Her daily woman has stopped. Stopped being daily, that is. Run away to join the circus out there, I imagine. You can't blame her. I do like your aunt, Alex, she came and talked to me in the bath. Aren't mothers supposed to do that? I never had one – I know now what I missed."

It seemed she was speaking to fill the space between them, pouring words out to keep something at bay, anxious eyes darting across his face.

She pulled him onto the sofa, jumping up to take another chair, a little apart, hands gently crossed in her lap, an ironic echo of the SOE interrogation pose.

As she straightened her gaunt shoulders she saw the glint in Alex's eyes and looked away. "It'll pass, love. Not enough to eat. I ought to feel ravenous, but I don't." She grinned, a skeleton face breaking his heart, "I know what – I shall let Captain Vere debrief me. Be warned, it's not a very flattering tale."

"You don't have to tell me anything. I can't even promise to listen, I just want to look. I'm happy enough just to sit here. Too happy, in fact."

"Oh, but there's things I have to explain. Things I owe you to say."

She shook away his protest, leaning towards him, resting her hand on his, leaving it there. "The look a little less intense, Captain, please. It unnerves. That day in London. I thought of you coming home and me not there."

Alex didn't reply. She seemed suddenly lost, staring at her feet, struggling for words.

"I'm a coward - that's what it comes to. No, don't interrupt ... I was going to tell you something that morning ... quite made up my mind to it. Then you were called to that damned meeting and I knew

132

they'd send you away. You'd be posted away, God knows where. Suddenly, everything seemed … what's the word? *Inopportune*. I couldn't … anyway, I didn't."

She stood up, pulling the robe tight at her waist, looking down at him, her expression a kind of reluctant pity. "So there you are. I ran away. I can't forgive myself for it. Only don't look so hurt, Alex, it doubles the wrong."

She managed a bright little smile, turning to walk away.

"Confession over. Now I must go and find some clothes, this robe is a scandal."

He called to her as she reached the door. "You mean the child don't you? That's what you were going to tell me."

She whirled round, holding on to the doorknob, swinging slightly to and fro, fearful dark eyes painfully searching for his.

"Yes …"

She let the silence hang between them, a brittle tentative smile flickering round her lips.

"Yes. That is what I meant. So you knew? Or guessed?"

Alex was about to speak when she cut across him. "It was those damned tulips wasn't it? Me coming back from Baker Street with my trophy flowers? I remember what you said. *Eternal love* – that was it. I couldn't bear you saying that. I knew what you would think, knew what we were in for. The two of us pretending … like both knowing you had a secret mistress. Something like that …"

She was weeping, tears running down to the crease of her mouth. She let them lie, staring him out, the tiny act of defiance tearing at his heart.

"No, no, you're wrong. I guessed nothing at all. I'm a naïve soul, Justine, you should know that. Gullible, if you like … but I'm not given to guessing. I suppose that's why I ended up with my job. No guessing allowed. All that *trust no one* stuff, remember?"

She looked at him, slowly nodding her head, "Then how …?"

"Lucile Beyrou told me."

*"Lucy?* How on earth? When did you ever meet her? But she promised ..."

"Don't blame her. I went to Dundee to see her. I tricked it out of her, let her think I knew more than I did. Interrogation tricks. I'm not very proud of my job."

She came across to the sofa, stumbling slightly, flopping down at his side. "If I don't sit somewhere, I'll fall over. Hold me, will you?"

She buried her face into his chest, her voice muffled. "He's a lovely boy, Alex. Really lovely. Our boy." She pulled away, her face very close, her eyes fixing his.

"Shall I say it again? Our boy. You'll see ..."

"You mean he's here? But ..."

"Not here, of course not. But I've got him safe alright."

She let him hold her close, two hands cupping his face, smiling into his eyes.

"All those months in that dreadful place. Knowing I would tell you this kept me alive. Even when I knew I'd never see you again, I would keep myself sane imagining telling you about little Pascal."

"I knew you'd choose that name. I mean, if it was a boy ..."

"Oh, of course a boy. So it was Lucy Beyrou? I don't mind. You can kiss me now. If you like. It seems opportune."

"That's why you left that ring behind, wasn't it? Lucile explained, but I'd already guessed. There - I can guess some things."

"She was a real soul mate in Dundee. The two of us comforting each other over our lost men, hatching our plans. I was sure I was going to stay there. Then these men turned up with the story about you in Paris. I suppose she told you?"

"Yes. But you knew I had never operated in Paris. It was certainly too late to start."

"Yes. Obviously a set-up. In fact, they barely tried to hide it. All the same I made the hell of a mistake. I tried to work out why. Why would anybody want to set me up? I forgot *why* is always the wrong question to ask. Trying to be too clever. God knows, I paid for asking it."

"It's only the wrong question because the victim never has any way of knowing. Tell me about these men. I can't help thinking John Cabot was involved. It was him shuffled me off to Scotland. I was well out of the way by then. But *Paris*?"

"Neither of them looked like him – not from the way you described him. No tubby Oxford chap with heavy glasses. They weren't the usual Baker Street issue at all. One was in Air Force uniform."

She squeezed his arm before he could speak, "Yes, I know, I know - uniforms are cheap. To tell the truth he was rather fetching, I do remember that much. You'd say a lady's man, except that sounds cheap. Actually he was very kind ... attentive and kind."

"You won't believe me, but I used to give lectures about that. In Torridon. Kindness can be a drug, a way of getting your brain to deny somebody is lying, even when it's obvious."

"They could see I was worked up because of you. That's what they kept playing on. You know - bringing news about Captain Vere, alive and kicking in Paris. Not that they were very specific."

"I was in Scotland."

"I was so relieved, even when I barely believed a word they said. That was what was clever - they could see I knew they were lying and they didn't care. They knew I was desperate to believe them."

"It's classic Cabot stuff."

"By the way, they knew the hell of a lot about our operations in the South West, me being captured, everything. Went on about how impressed they were. They knew a lot of detail. Too much, now I think about it. Once or twice, I thought they might be fishing about Gliess, but I'm probably wrong – you really couldn't say they were pumping me. Thinking back, I realise they were being quite clever, you know, making flattering conversation. Why hadn't I been decorated? Stupid things like that."

"This man Cabot is dangerous. He was involved. I'll stake my life on it. Schemes like that were his speciality - long range killing."

"But it wasn't a scheme, Alex – it really wasn't. And why would he go to the trouble of snaring me? Why would he do that?"

"You're asking why again. It won't do. Cabot thought I'd told you something deadly secret. Or rather that I *could* have told you something - same thing, as far as he's concerned. A hell of lot rested on that secret. If they thought you knew too much ... You didn't, of course. That's why it's pointless to ask why."

"They let drop they'd lost contact with you. Just said they'd lost contact with your Paris cell. This was just before they left. They didn't seem too concerned. I didn't imagine they'd come back."

"And you spent the following days getting more and more agitated, worrying about my mysterious cell being out of contact. I'm right, aren't I?"

"I suppose so. But they seemed so clueless, Alex, as if they didn't care all that much. It's hard to credit all that was a lie."

"No point of lying if you're no good at it."

"But you were right. They did come back. That was a few days later. By then I was so worried they could have persuaded me to anything. All I got were frustrating hints that you were still out of contact. One of them said the problem was none of the Paris circuits knew Captain Vere by sight."

"Making everything the usual cock-up, agents lost in the fog of war. God, where have I seen that one before?"

"I heard them say it would be too risky to send a courier who didn't know you by sight. I realised they were going to abandon you."

"So Justine Perry volunteered, resigned or not. You're right, it was clever, even by Cabot's standards. They had you either way. After all, you'd operated in the occupied zone, you knew Paris. You knew me."

"No need to look like that. Looked at that way, they were right. I was the ideal person to send. Resignation didn't come into it."

"Ideal, except for the minor matter that I wasn't in Paris. Let me guess the rest. Along comes this extraordinarily coincidental chance to get you in."

Justine nodded, a tiny rueful smile. "Don't sound so superior, Alex. I'm ashamed, but only because of how gullible they thought I was. It was humiliating."

"I know that feeling. I've known it all my life."

"They got me across on a fishing boat into Brittany two nights later. I was passed from one safe house to the next. I suppose they thought the pass-the-parcel business would blind me to what I was walking into."

"Which was?"

"I ended up thinking I'd somehow been kidnapped. Perhaps that's not the right word ... somehow I'd ended up back in France. The last place on God's earth I should be. Velvet handcuffs, you know. It was then I decided I had to get out. I remember I was fiddling with a WT set one night. This French chap – they were all French – started barking at me to leave it alone. That was when I realised I was pretty well a prisoner."

"Where was this? Close to Paris?"

"I can tell you exactly. They said it was the final leg. Outside Drieu. Everybody was jumpy that night because the escort was so late. Then this awful shifty woman arrived. Kept going on about when she was going to be paid. That night I caught her going through my kit. She said she was looking for money and backed off, but I knew I was pretty well trapped."

"And once you were arrested, you would disappear in a cloud of glory doing a job you'd volunteered for. Volunteered, way beyond any call of duty. Everything you ever knew would go with you. Nobody would be responsible. That's how he works."

"You mean this Cabot chap? But I wasn't arrested. At least, not then. I slipped away while the escort was out scouting for breakfast, walked to the railway station and bought a ticket for Nantes."

"*Nantes*?" Alex was smiling. "You mean a switch?"

"I counted on them panicking, thinking I'd done something reckless. Once I'd bought the ticket I walked back into the village and caught the bus to Caumont. I shouldn't have got away with it, but I did. You have to be unlucky to have your papers checked on a bus. In fact a man helped me on board. You're forgetting I had a card to play."

He found himself blushing.

"Being pregnant is a passport in France, you know that. A suitcase would have been even better, but I had my little shopping basket. The driver took my sous, kept everybody waiting until I was settled."

"*Caumont*. I've never heard of the place What's there?"

"A school. Well, actually it's a convent, but it's a school as well. It was my old school. It wasn't far to walk."

"You mean they took you in, just like that? They'd take that risk?"

"I wish I could say all for the sake of my blue eyes. But it was money, of course. Before the war the Convent used to accept paying visitors, people looking for a retreat. All that had stopped. One thing you can say about SOE, they don't stint on cash."

"If it was French money we probably printed it."

"They took it all the same, and kept quiet. That's where little Pascal was born. You can do worse than be born in a convent."

She pressed Alex's hand against her cheek. "Don't look so solemn, Guffin. It was all perfectly satisfactory. One of the Sisters was a midwife. We managed. The nuns were kind and I had our little boy. Apart from wondering where you were, things could have been worse."

"And that's where he is now? This convent?"

"Pascal? Say his name, Alex. No, he's not there. It didn't take long for the rumours to start. Babies are hard to ignore in a convent. One day the Mother Superior told us she'd been denounced. Two letters apparently, both from the same person. The usual stuff - the convent was a sink of depravity, the Archbishop was coupling with the nuns, half the nuns were pregnant, and so forth. Not very inventive, but the poor woman couldn't let it pass. She offered to hide Pascal if I took myself off."

For a moment he thought she had stopped. She sat looking round the room as if searching for something.

"Perhaps I'd have made a different decision ... if they had given me more time." Something desperate in her voice made him look away.

"I haven't seen him since that morning."

"But he's safe?"

There were lines on her face he had never seen before. Faint pencil marks of strain, tightening as she turned to him.

"I believe so. Please don't ask me, please not. I don't dare say. Forgive me, my love. If they take me, I will die easily rather than say. I can't ask that of you. Yes, they say he is perfectly safe." She remembered something, suddenly smiling. "There's a little garden. I like to think of him in a garden."

Alex went to the window, stepping out onto the balcony. The sun had almost gone, the air suddenly damp.

He called through to her: "Everywhere is very quiet. It's like the whole place is waiting for something. Not a soul anywhere. Just a car the other side of the street. Nobody inside. It looks abandoned. I suppose you were picked up at the railway station? You must have known you didn't stand a chance."

She waited until he came back inside, settling himself close to her on the sofa. "Bus station actually. I walked to the village and was standing waiting in the little shelter at the *arrêt*. It's always the little things isn't it, Guffin. I didn't know Thursday was Market Day. They shift the bus stop somewhere else. It was a dreadful mistake. Nobody said anything, of course. I was too well dressed for one thing. Just kept looking at me standing there with my little case as if I was mad. In the end, a local police chap came up and asked was I going to stand there all day because the bus didn't come until half past seven. Not much of a policeman – the one they sent to collect money from the stall-holders. It's always the little things, isn't it? He asked for my papers. Asked why I'd come shopping when my card was six months out of date. Had I been living in a cave? He had that stupid determined look, like a dog with a bone. I knew it was all up."

## seventeen

"THEY took me to the Drancy transit camp. In a bus – quite civilised as arrests go."

She lay stretched out on the sofa, clutching the glass of water he had forced into her hands, staring into it now and then, as if surprised to find it there.

"It's like a madhouse in there. You get called up one by one. In front of trestle tables - a bit like standing at the Post Office. They had my papers spread out, two women squabbling about what they called my *situation*. They asked a man to arbitrate on the Nuremberg Laws ... well, the French ones. I might have been a sick dog on its last trip to the vet. It's an insane version of The Last Judgement. In my case, God was a little French chap with very bad breath."

"The Jewish Laws?"

"He was perfectly polite about it. It was as if he didn't really believe what he was doing. I was supposed not to care whether they put me down or not. I'll always remember how polite everybody was, thumbing through your papers, thinking what best to do with you."

She suddenly pulled away from him.

"Do you really want to hear this, Alex? I haven't thought about it for ages. Bringing it all back makes me tired. I'll end up weeping."

"You don't have to explain anything. Not to me. All I care about is you're here. Why don't you get some rest? We have to talk to Madeleine when she gets back – it's dangerous staying here, you realise that?"

"It doesn't feel dangerous. No, I'll sleep later. I owe it to all those poor devils who got sent away. Talking about it just made me lose heart somehow. All this sleep has made me weak. The truth is after I was arrested I barely believed what was happening. There I was in an ugly housing estate in Paris, people discussing whether I deserved to stay alive. What they did seemed so ordinary, you see. They hand you a little slip of coloured paper and tell you to take it to another table.

She was struggling for words, biting her finger like a child finding itself caught with a secret.

"The Jews always got a purple slip."

"I don't understand … a purple slip?"

"A little purple slip of paper. Nothing else. Hundreds of people arrived every day at Drancy. You'd imagine people would ask why the camp was never full - they never did. There … I've lost my thread."

"A purple paper …"

"Yes. You get one of those and wait your turn for the train to Pitchipoi. No Pitchipoi for me - I always got another chance to live. Every time. Always a red slip, never purple."

"Pitchipoi?"

"It's what the Jewish children call the place the trains go to. You hear mothers talking about it to their kids. Trying to calm them down … you know … giving them something to look forward to."

Something was breaking in her voice, her eyes tormented, staring at him as if she barely knew him. "For heaven's sake, you know what I'm talking about. The Polish camps. Slaughter houses. Children clutching their little purple slips for the slaughter house. I'm not sure I can talk about this. It's disgusting. Do you know why I wasn't purple, Alex? Can you guess why? It's almost comic."

Alex shook his head, looking away, "But you're not Jewish ..."

"Of course I was Jewish."

"You mean your papers? London would never make that mistake."

"No, not our people in London, not Baker Street. But I wouldn't say the same for that French lot in Duke Street – they could easily have made the papers that woman in Drieu switched on me. It was all she needed to do. Drancy would see to the rest. I was bound to be deported. God, why am I using that word? *Killed*, that's the word. One Jew the less, except ..."

She stared him down, a defiant flush on her face, "My state ... given my state. Whoever faked those papers thought it better I was married. I can just see some spotty clerk thinking that one up. Circumstantial colour. That's always the problem, isn't it? I remember you saying how people always over-egg things. Certain people can't resist being clever. I ended up with a whole wallet of papers - husband, marriage certificate, family photographs, the lot."

"You forget I was one of those spotty clerks. That's what we did in the TPSU. Working with Cabot. We spent months inventing German officers."

"That's why I don't think it was Baker Street. Whoever did it, didn't check. Short of time, I suppose. The dead husband they saddled me with wasn't so dead. His name turned up on a list of captured combatants in the Russian campaign. He had been logged as a POW. Decorated, what's more. That's the joke. They had managed to marry me to a serving soldier ..."

"I can't see what difference ..."

"... to an Ayrian serving soldier. I told you – the Nuremberg Laws. I suppose it saves their sanity – they pretend it's all about the law. It says you can't deport wives of POWs even if they're Jewish. So I ended up with a red slip every time. That's how I came to be in the Lévitan store. They couldn't gas me, but there was no reason why they shouldn't work me to death."

Alex pulled her close, aware of the fragility of her body, taking her head between his hands, tentatively tracing the outline of the bruise on her cheek.

"It's alright, I know."

She shook her head, pushing him away, "No, Alex, you don't know. Things are not always the way you imagine them."

"Bruises like this don't just appear."

"Nobody hit us. It wasn't like that. I got the bruise lifting a crate. That's what we do most of the time, shift crates about. Something fell out on top of me - a piano stool I think. Half knocked me out. I was told off, because I held things up, but that's all. The guards won't come anywhere near us. They're a funny lot. Mongolian, I think. Very superstitious. You catch them eying you as if you were sacred somehow, the way people look at dying patients in hospital. Not so far off the truth when you think about it."

She leaned towards him, the kiss no more than a touch, her lips dry against his face. "That's for a start. Now I don't want to talk about me any more. Can't we talk about you? Or not talk at all. I can just be here. We don't even need to speak. I was thinking in the bath there's only so much relief a body can take. Too much, and you start to feel queer. I do feel a bit queer. Can't I just be quiet and look at you? I'm tired of questions."

"Just one question. I don't understand how you ended up in that church."

"Madeleine said she told you. About that priest."

"I remember she said people sometimes got food from the church. Nothing else."

"So the question is why *you* ended up there."

"It was a woman in an art shop. Madeleine's friend. She knew about the church handing out food. She told me to go there. I'd wasted most of the day watching the front of the shop. It seemed hopeless."

"Two weeks ago they stopped delivering food to the store. There were days when nothing arrived at all. There's a sort of camp committee. We proposed they let us out overnight, those that could get food. Brunner refused at first then changed his mind. He started sorting people into groups. Women and old men first. They gave us this paper to take to the Prefecture tomorrow."

"Madeleine says the men left behind have already been deported. Herr Brunner is filling one last convoy."

"You only got these *Quittance* forms if you had family who would feed you. Somebody said I should tell them I was going to the soup kitchen at my church. I told the priest I'd been working in the Lévitan store. I suppose I looked so dreadful he took pity on me. So I got some bread and honey. His own honey - he keeps bees. He's an odd sort of priest."

"I heard his sermon. He went on as if it was 1848 all over again, only this time it would be different. The usual stuff, the end of the ruling class and so forth. It was dreadfully careless talk – he was taking the hell of a risk."

"Not as much as you think. The food hand-outs are just a cover. He's quite a big fish in the Communist Party. He knows exactly how far he can go. The Vichy people leave him alone. They think he's just a barmy old crank. A mistake. He already knew about the plan to empty the Lévitan store. About Brunner rounding up all the forced labour, Jewish or not. One last insane convoy. There's a cache of small arms in the church. For the *Front National* when the uprising starts. Not long, he said."

"Small arms against half a dozen German brigades. He must be mad."

It was evening before Madeleine returned, dumping her empty basket on the hall floor, standing looking at them, blinking herself into a show of recognition.

As Alex took her coat she brushed him away, sinking into a chair, sitting immobile, staring at him, her face like chalk.

"You remember that meeting? The night you arrived. After they shot that informer I knew there'd be hell to pay. They're so naïve. Boys, that's all they are. They don't believe anybody would betray them. They've been listening to that fool de Gaulle going on about *mobilising a fighting force*. As if there was even a war to fight. It's completely mad. Fighting with what? All we have is a few hand guns. There's a young chap called Marc. I suppose you'd call him the leader, not that they believe in leaders. He said he was organising the first patrol. In the Bois de Boulogne."

Justine fetched her a glass of brandy. Madeleine looked at it in her hand, forgetting to drink.

"I warned them you can't trust anybody in Paris. Shooting that woman was a mistake. They went off like schoolboys on a trip to the Bois. Twenty or more. Of course, the Gestapo were waiting. We've a new Governor. Only been here a few weeks. Called von Choltitz. He's responsible for all the explosives everywhere. He doesn't believe in prisoners. The first thing he did was ship off all the resistance in prison to a place called Dachau. It's sure they'll all be killed when they get there. Like my boys … Marc was the only one who got away. I talked to him when he got back. He said they'd tried to run but they were between two machine guns. I think most of them are dead."

She stood up, handing the glass back to Justine, walking wearily into the salon. She slumped into a chair, closing her eyes. She looked old.

"Are you there Alex? Come here. There's something I need to tell you. I have a dreadful headache. I must rest my eyes."

Justine kneeled down by her chair, one arm round her shoulders.

"You should lie down. Go and rest, I will make us something to eat."

"Alex, can you hear? I was hoping to ask Marc about somewhere safe for the two of you. Impossible. I saw him when he got back. God help him."

"That's the chap who got away?"

"They always see there's someone who gets away. It breaks morale. If you get away you must have been an informer. I can't believe Marc betrayed them, but who am I to say that? When I told him he was best to lie low he said I was accusing him."

She shook her head, looking from Alex to Justine, "I suppose I was. Anyway, it's not a risk we can take now. We had to get you away and Marc was my best hope ... my only hope."

She glanced across to the open window, the sky jet-black outside.

"Perhaps one more night. It seems quiet enough. If there's a raid on the building, at least we'll hear them coming."

Alex looked at Justine. Neither spoke.

# eighteen

THEY were sitting in the kitchen when they heard the sound at the door. Not even a knock, more a soft scraping double tap. Alex reached out, his hand on top of Justine's, pressing it to the table.

Madeleine stiffened, her head cocked.

At the second scratch at the door she relaxed. "It's alright, I know who it is." She was whispering.

"We use a sort of code in the building, just in case. It's the woman from the floor below. Asking about bread, I dare say. I can't help her much."

She looked at Justine, her voice suddenly urgent. "Go and sit in the salon. Not a sound. If she wants to come in, I usually bring her in here. Alex, come with me, the sight of a man will keep her quiet for weeks."

Alex watched as Madeleine peered through the little spy-hole. Her shoulders relaxed.

"Yes, it's her." He heard the relief in her voice. "She's a dreadful gossip, don't say more than you have to."

She slipped the chain and pulled the door open.

The woman was already scuttling away, heavy black skirt trailing down the marble stairs. Two men pressed against the wall on either side filled the doorframe, closing ranks, pushing inside past Madeleine. Standard milice uniform: tight black jersey, brown leather bandolier, heavy, iron-clad boots.

"You have a worker from the Lévitan here."

A tiny wiry man, wrinkled simian face the colour of walnuts. He seemed too old for this work, resting his rifle on the parquet as if the weight were too much.

He flapped an outstretched hand to a boy at his side – gangly, awkward, warily eyeing Madeleine. He could not have been more than sixteen, hurriedly pulling a crumpled bit of yellow paper from his pocket, pushing it into the old man's hand.

He passed it to Madeleine, snatching it back as she shook her head. "Suit yourself. It's a warrant. Hurry up - we don't have all night. Where is she?" Madeleine ignored him, stretching a hand out to the youth, letting it drop as he flinched away.

"It's Thierry isn't it? How's your mother getting on? It's been a long time. Are you still living …"

"… I don't know her." A strained hysterical squeak, eyes darting to the older man. "I've not seen her before, honest. You back off, old woman. What d'you know about my mother?"

Alex walked towards the old man opening his cigarette case, holding it out.

"It looks like you've come to the wrong place. You're welcome to look round." He laughed, "Mind you, does it look like we have escaped prisoners …"

The man ignored the cigarettes, following Alex's eyes out into the stairwell, kicking the door closed behind him. He waited for the echo to die in the space outside.

"And who might you be? As if we didn't know. You got papers?"

"I'll fetch them."

149

"No you won't. You'll stay where you are … and don't think I won't use this."

He turned again to Madeleine, tiny eyes suddenly savage. "Are you going to fetch her or do we start looking?"

Alex lit a cigarette, walking past him. "This is stupid. You've come to the wrong place."

"Have we then? Next time you go to church, remember to put some money in the box. People notice things like that. D'you imagine we're all stupid? You were followed all the way to your little nest."

"She's not here I tell you ... there's nobody here. You're making …"

The blow to his shin was executed so casually that for a moment he was uncertain how the pain arose. Alex staggered against the side table, watching impotently as the vase tottered over the edge. Freesias scattered across the floor as it smashed. Madeleine stooped down, abandoning the effort as the man lifted the butt of the rifle, prodding her shoulder.

"Leave it. We're in a hurry. Fetch the woman … fetch her … or it'll be more than a china pot."

*"Who is it, Madeleine?"*

They had not heard Justine come in. She stood in the salon doorway holding out a sheet of paper.

"I heard you asking. Is this what you want? It's my *Quittance* from the Lévetan store. It's all perfectly in order."

The old man took it, crumpling it into his pocket. "I don't know anything about that. You're to come with us. You'll need your coat for the star."

"They gave me a red slip."

He waved the warrant in her face, smoothing it out, squinting down at the few lines of print.

"Listen, Madame Fortieu, you can sing your song when we get there. You're wasting our time. It says here they want you back." He whirled round, confronting Alex.

"You. Papers. I asked for your papers."

"And I said I'll get them."

"Stay where you are." He brandished the warrant at Madeleine, forcing it too close to her face. "It says you live on your own. If you'd bothered to read it. *Sole Occupant* – know what that means? Who's he?"

"My nephew. Just staying the night."

"I've never seen him before. He's not from round here ..." The boy's stage whisper was for Madeleine's benefit. "We should take her as well. She's a liar."

"Oh yes, why not take the lot of them?" The old man was laughing at him, "I'll tell you why not, son. There's not enough room in the bloody car."

He slung the rifle over his shoulder, throwing the warrant down onto the table, shrugging at Madeleine.

"You - report to the Prefecture tomorrow. Take that with you. Him - he comes with us. Thierry, go with him, get his papers."


It took a long time to get the engine started, filling the inside of the tiny car with smoke, the smell reminding Alex of Inverness. He was pushed inside hard against Justine, the schoolboy leering nervously at them over the back of his seat, fumbling left-handed with the catch of a pistol, pushing it up and down, the thing absurdly big in his hand.

Approaching the junction, the car stopped. The old man got out, bending back inside for his rifle.

"Keep an eye on them. I'm going to see."

"See what?" Kneeling on his seat, the boy craned round peering through the windscreen.

One of the platanes at the crossroads was sprawled on its side across the road, dusty leaves rearing into the night air.

"What's going on?"

"See for yourself. Road's blocked. The bastards have started cutting the trees down."

The old man got back in, poking his rifle into the well between the two seats.

"We'll have to go round. It's alright, I know the way."

"It says you can't go down here. There's a sign."

"Who's to stop us, then?

The road widened out between cliffs of grey stone apartments. A fairground smell of hot food blew briefly through the open windows.

Justine leaned against Alex, her lips to his ear, "I know where we are. I know where he's taking us."

Alex pressed his cheek against hers, feeling it wet.

"What's that they're talking, Boris?"

The boy sounded scared, kneeling up, leaning over the back of his seat, fat beads of sweat glistening on his face.

"That's English. They're talking English."

The old man darted a glance behind, catching Justine's eye.

She stared back at him, shouting in German: "Take a good look imbecile."

He prodded the youth at his side, grinning, "Get down from there - she bites. And stop waving that bloody thing about. They can talk what they like. Look, we're here now. Straighten up. Have you got the paper?"

They had turned sharply left down a steep ramp, pulling up behind a removal van parked for the night. A huge fire blazed at one end of a paved courtyard, green flames licking round bits of broken furniture. Showers of sparks leapt into the night sky as a man tossed a child's high chair onto the fire, painted roses melting as it burned.

Two soldiers in uniform came out of a tunnel of darkness beyond the fire, walking slowly towards them. A German officer at a side door stood waiting for them, reaching to switch on a single electric lamp under a metal shade set in the wall. They gathered round the car peering into the back seat.

The officer glanced at the driver's warrant, passing a wad of banknotes through the open window, waiting impatiently while the old man counted them.

One of the soldiers opened the back doors filling the car with the scent of wood smoke. Nobody spoke.

Justine's hand grazed his own as Alex let the solders shepherd them down a long sloping corridor to an open door at the far end. A hub-hub of agitated voices dipped momentarily as they came in.

Forty or more people were crammed into a tiny anteroom. Unlikely prisoners, the men were mostly in dinner jackets, the women in evening dress. An improbable pall of cigar smoke hung over the hot little room.

A tall woman carrying a fur wrap broke away from a group, fighting her way through the crush.

"Oh, Justine, my dear girl, you as well. I knew they'd never let us go. I knew it. But not so soon. You see how things are. I was walking through the Luxembourg this afternoon. Dead. All the shops closed. Even the cafés – shutters up everywhere. No police, just soldiers everywhere. I've never seen so many. And the metro. I walked down the steps just to look. Platforms packed with angry Germans. They looked as if they'd been there for hours, you could hardly see for smoke. The Luxembourg is always full of police, nice boys, gossiping. Somebody said they've been disarmed, so they're on strike. Can the police do that? That's what brought the Germans on the streets."

She pressed the back of one hand to her cheek, a curious theatrical gesture, widening her eyes.

"I knew that madman would never let us go, but this … He's mad."

Justine stepped back, as if the woman's hysteria were somehow infectious.

153

"Who's mad? I don't know anything. I've been asleep for a day or more. All I know is a couple of milice came to the apartment. They just ignored my *Quittance*." She turned to Alex, managing a thin little smile, "Alex, this is a fellow Lévitan inmate. Madame … Oh, no. Can I?"

"What? My name?" The woman laughed. "Of course you can tell him. I'm Cecile Arbout." She stared into Alex's face, finally swivelling a crooked smile back to Justine. "It's no use, my dear, he's never heard of me." Resting one hand on Alex's arm, briefly leaving it there. "You're forgiven. A long time ago I was in films. You're too young." The sudden bark of a laugh - too loud - brought faces turning to look. "God in heaven … everybody's too young to remember that."

She pressed one hand against his shoulder, her face close enough for him to smell her perfume – something hot and flowery. "Our German friends don't know. Between you and me, Germans and actresses don't mix. Strange expectations, as we used to say. You think I'm going to risk that at my age?"

She stepped back, making an odd little curtsey, grabbing him to steady herself. "I'm a seamstress now, believe it or not."

Something in her voice made him look away.

She turned to Justine, her eyes wild. "I think I've offended him. Here, young man, let the seamstress tell you all about our dress-making department. We have a really wonderful tailor." She was gabbling - a rush of hysterical words beating into his ear. "Jewish, of course. Germans don't believe in tailors unless they are Jewish."

Justine reached out, taking her hand, squeezing it, "It's alright, Cecile, it's alright."

"Bespoke suiting for the men ... did I say that? *Haute couture* for the women, of course. Even Madame von Behr … can you imagine that? Really wonderful stuff. And all completely free … completely free …isn't that a miracle?"

She had pulled Alex round, her face close to his. For a moment she looked insane. Seeing something in his eyes, she turned away, drawing hard on a long-extinguished cigarette.

"This damned thing's dead." Her voice was suddenly calmer. "Do you have a cigarette, young man? I'm sorry. Did you think I was mad? It was the disappointment, you see. They rounded up my celebration party. Celebrating my release, can you believe? My theatre crowd."

"But rounded up for what?" It was all he could think of saying. He saw her anxious face as people turned to his voice.

"Not so loud." Justine was whispering. "For God's sake don't attract attention. Sometimes there's a plant to listen in."

She pulled again at Cecile's hand: "You were going to explain about Brunner. What's this about Brunner?"

"You missed him. Our leader said he wants to check all our papers again. He actually deigned to walk among us. This was before you arrived. Stood on one of the ladders to give a little speech. We're to go back to Drancy to have it done."

Alex felt the heat of her breath again in his ear. "I'm not Jewish you know. We all say this, but it's true. I've always been a non-deportable – lovely expression, isn't it?"

She had fallen silent, eyebrows raised, inspecting him, the expression too knowing to be comfortable. For a moment he thought she was waiting for him to say something but she simply stood, idly rubbing one hand against the other, apparently finding the action reassuring.

"You know the little theatre on the rue Saint Germain?" It seemed she was seeing him for the first time, a smile suddenly embracing him. "It's my husband's. They took him away ... all this was a long time ago. Two Gendarmes came for him. Very smart. I remember it was a Saturday ... perhaps they didn't care about that. I recall they saluted him – it seemed ridiculous. I haven't heard from him since. You know, when it started, Henri would read things out of the newspaper. *Not in Paris*, he'd say. I can hear him saying it now."

She freed herself from Justine's hand. "Yes ... about Herr Brunner. A woman over there heard they started loading this afternoon. All the young men in the store. They were taken in a bus to the marshalling yard at the *Gare Austerlitz*. Do you think it's true? That damned maniac and his convoys."

"But the Americans ..." Realising she was not listening, Alex tried again, "The Americans ... I mean ..."

"*Americans*?" She looked puzzled. "What about Americans? You think Americans are interested in his convoys? Are you so sure? I think they will say *if that's what you French want, what business is it of ours*? Why should they stop it?"

Sweat was running in lines down to the corners of her mouth completing the disintegration of her make-up.

As she walked away he heard her mutter to Justine, *your young man seems very naïve.*


A guard pushed into the sweating crowd, making space, dumping piles of old clothes on the floor. Alex watched as people dipped down, looking for things, snatching particular bits out of the pile. Women deep in conversation barely paused, slipping coarse striped aprons over their heads.

Cecile stood catching her breath before straightening a crude sacking tabard round her shoulders. A huge yellow star was sewed to the breast.

A group of old men began plucking grubby overalls from a pile, awkwardly helping each other to pull them on.

Alex felt Justine's cheek brush his own, her whisper urgent. "It looks like they're going to make us work. Pray God it won't be all night. You'll need something to wear. Just take what's left. Look natural."

He dawdled to the back of the line, pulling something like a child's smock from the bottom of the pile and struggling into it. He followed the others and began sorting through numbered armbands strewn across a trestle table. As he picked one it was snatched from his hand.

"Mine, I think." The man at his side fished down into the pile, a chocolate theatre voice rumbling in Alex's ear, the accent impeccable.

"How about this? Poor chap won't miss it now."

An odd expectant silence had fallen on the room. Without any specific command they formed lines like obedient children, standing two by two as double doors at the far end of the room were flung back.

It seemed he had walked into a nightmare. The limitless space of a cavernous hall. Line upon line of feeble electric lamps dangling over a kind of madman's jumble sale. An exhibition consumed by its own excess: rows of tables set out with ghostly piles of starched linen: sheets, table-cloths, napkins, pillow-cases, towels, curtains, eiderdowns, bed-spreads. Everywhere the overpowering smell of damp cloth.

Wooden crates stood waiting between the tables.

"This was my room."

Justine seemed not to realise she was already lifting towels from the pile, practised hands folding them flat. "Watch what I do. It's more organised than it looks. Only towels in this crate. They check."

She looked up, tears filling the dark eyes that met his own, lost to some familiar misery.

"God forgive me, Alex. I've dragged you into hell."

# nineteen

THE chime of something like a school bell from the room above brought an end to work, a sudden surge of chatter breaking hours of silence. Linen lay abandoned where it fell, people slumping exhausted to the floor.

Alex perched awkwardly on the edge of a crate, breathing the fresh scent of cigarettes. An old man re-lit the stump of a cigar. From somewhere behind a tower of wicker baskets someone was banging a door, shouting *let me in. I need a bucket.*

Alex followed Justine across to a space on the floor where the windows had been boarded up. He sank down alongside her, his back against the wall. She seemed already asleep, the familiar tremor flickering across her face.

She opened her eyes as he touched her hair, a tiny smile turning his heart over.

"Hello Guffin. No, not asleep – just warding off misery."

"Cecile. The actress. You heard what she said?"

Something in his face made her turn away, confused, feeling for his hand, pulling it to her body, holding it tight.

"Shall I tell you something? There used to be children in the Lévitan store – you didn't know that? Of course, you didn't. Nobody will ever know. You heard them running about. They used to play on the floor upstairs ... where they fix the clocks. One day Herr Brunner announced it wasn't a safe place for children. I suppose it was his idea of a joke. Let them all go to Pitchipoi ... that's what it came to. Can you think God made men like that? Can you?"

There was something dangerous in her voice. Alex pressed her hand, stroking it, desperately willing her away from some desperate edge. She freed herself, sitting quiet, head slumped down on her chest.

"The day they took the children away I thought a lot about Pascal. Normally I ration that ... you understand? I couldn't stop thinking of them locked in the waggons at Austerlitz. It was the only time I cried. I was ashamed – but you weep for children, don't you? What else? We watched them lined up in the yard. They were so small."

She shuddered, leaning against him, shaking her head. "And I've brought you to this. I wish to God you hadn't found me."

He pressed her hand to his lips, tears starting to his eyes, "Quiet my love, don't say any more. I want to sit and think for a bit. I'll have to do it for both of us."

"*Think?* You mean about getting out? That's all we did in the early days. You think, this is Paris - how hard can it be to walk out of a shop? That's the rue Saint-Denis just outside. Sometimes when it's quiet you can hear the trains in the station. But it's a waste of time, Alex. Nobody has ever got out. Well, apart from Sylvie. The guards are locked in with us. If we get to them, we all die."

She had fallen silent, her eyes closed. Alex pulled at her hand. "Don't sleep yet ... we have to talk."

"Not talk about escape, my love. I've already had all that talk – months of it. It always comes down to the same thing – die now, or wait your turn."

There was a commotion as a door was opened on the other side of the room, a sudden crush of people milling to get out. Justine struggled to stand, falling against him with an exasperated sigh.

"Hell, I'm so weak. They've opened the back stairs up to crockery and silverware. There might be something to eat."

She tottered back, steadying herself against the wall. "It's no good. I'll stay here. You go. There are a few camp beds up there."

"You think I'd leave you? Remember how I carried you on my back that time making for the safe house at Saint Aunix? Do I have to do it again? Come on, lean on me."

She let him pull her upright, leaning unsteadily against him, her breath coming hard.

"You're a noble soul, Guffin. What did I ever do to deserve you? I was just feeling sorry for myself. You're right, we should get out of the stink. People have started using the buckets in here. It's the bastards' way of keeping you down - nothing like squatting over a bucket to humiliate you."


The floor above exchanged linen for mantle clocks, crockery, and glassware. China ornaments jostled together on avenues of trestle tables. Vases and pottery had been laid out on wider tables with sad little piles of photograph frames stacked face down. Towers of metal cooking pans leaned out from half-filled crates.

A stained blue carpet in one corner was spread with cutlery neatly sorted in sets: knives, forks, spoons, crudely tied together in bundles with bits of string.

Unsure where to go, Alex found himself stumbling against a wicker laundry basket stuffed with crockery, the plates on top alive with the glistening amber shells of feasting cockroaches.

Justine pulled him back. "It's where you put the things that still have food on them. It's not been emptied for days. I remember the first time I found food. I was rummaging in my crate, pulling things out. And there was somebody's breakfast. Still set out on its plate. It used to break my heart thinking that's when everything ended for somebody. They wouldn't have thought their life would end up here with us picking over it."

160

She held up one of a pair of silver candlesticks. "Pretty. You have to put anything that looks like silver to one side. It goes to be polished up for the display room downstairs, the lobby they call it. All the good stuff goes there. It's set out like in a regular shop, even cash registers – not that they work. Von Behr's wife shops there. *Shops* – that's how she puts it. As if she thinks it's less like theft done that way, less like armed robbery. Can you understand people like that? Greedy little children playing shops. I worked down in the lobby for a week, boxing things up for an officer's wife. They were furnishing their apartment. It was supposed to be a privilege working there. I was sent back up here to pack linen, for looking insolent."

An upright piano, thick in dust, had been pushed against the wall, next to stacks of frying pans, a single sheet of music entangled in its broken fretwork stand. Alex pulled it away. A child's study by Czerny, the fingering picked out in pencil. Somebody had written, *Try to get more legato in the left hand Patrice*, across the top with the date of the next lesson. June the ninth. Two years ago.

Justine took his hand, standing next to him, answering his thoughts.

"It's not that people didn't care. It took me a long time to realise that. Paris can't afford to care. The people made that choice years ago. In Paris it's always us or them."

"Which are we?"

She leaned across to read the label pasted on the lid of the piano.

"It was a mistake. Pianos shouldn't come to Lévitan. They're supposed to go to the Palais de Tokyo. Don't look at me like that, Alex. How can I answer you? What would you do? Would you have the courage to make the right choice? Life always seems very precious."

Alex waved his arm into the dusty air. "Here's what happens when you look the other way. This is how it always ends."

"And the people made to do this hideous job? Hundreds and hundreds of us. You work until one morning you can't get up.

Nothing dramatic. They take you to the hospital. Good word, *hospital*. It sounds restful. Soon there won't be enough of us left. Nobody will remember what happened because there will be nobody to do the remembering. Paris decided it would be convenient not to know. A city with a hole in its memory."

Alex realised he was still holding the scrap of music. Trying to perch it back onto the music stand it slipped down. He watched impotently as it fluttered off like a paper aeroplane, coming to rest under a chest of drawers. He left it where it lay.

"Is there water somewhere? I'm very thirsty."

"A tap by the buckets. But it's usually turned off. Water is their favourite punishment ... that and night work. We've been lucky - the bell means they're not going to make us sort all night."

She found a place on the floor, sliding down, her back against the wall.

"Come and sit with me, Guffin. When they turn the lights off, it's pitch black. I don't want to lose you. We're quiet enough here. There's nothing to do but wait."

"Wait for what?"


The lights had been cut an hour ago, the click of some master switch reminding Alex of the church in the *Passage*. He stared into the darkness, trying to orient himself, imagining the narrow winding lane beyond the walls of the shop. It could not be so very far - that church. Only a few yards as the crow flies. The priest would have gone home by now.

Voices echoed up the stairwell, men calling to each other, no more than an amiable exchange of banter. The rattle of an opening door brought the smell of fresh tobacco, bright torchlight projecting shadows from towers of candlesticks, heavy boots clumping between the crates. They were counting bodies.

As the door banged shut, one of the men called out in a language Alex did not recognise, bringing an echoing reply from somewhere far away. The two men were laughing together in the corridor outside, moving slowly away.

Alex lay alongside Justine, gently pulling her close, listening to the tiny sounds of huddled humanity around him, knowing sleep would never come.

In the dead of the night Cecile's voice querulously cut someone short, a theatrical whisper echoing in the darkness. *No you old fool, you're not coming back. We're for the pit.*

Justine stirred, reaching out to him enclosing him, her voice in his ear part of the velvet dark. "Alex, love, I've been dreaming about that ring. I feel guilty there wasn't a proper goodbye. You knew, didn't you? About the ring?"

"That there was only us. Just us. Nobody else. That's nothing to be guilty about."

"I'd never loved anyone. Doesn't that sound shocking? Nothing ever like that for me until I met my Guffin. Took me by surprise." He felt her stir, her lips seeking his. "I mean a happy surprise. That and our little Pascal. Two of you in one go."

"You should have told me all the same."

"Is that a reproach?" He heard the smile in her voice. "No, my love, that's the one thing I'm sure of. I wasn't going to have you fret your days away thinking what if it's not mine. Best think nothing at all than think all that sordid stuff."

Holding her tight against him he could think of no reply, bright images of a little boy flooding his mind. Watching a tiny figure, head bowed, earnestly consumed by the intensity of play. Him standing somewhere he had yet to know. A garden perhaps.

Her breath against his cheek came easily now. "You still haven't asked, Alex. Not right out. When I knew about Pascal. You remember the Russell Hotel? The night we lay in bed and watched that raid? I could have eaten you that night, quite gobbled you up. Did you not know? It was then. The next morning. Long before that monster Gliess. I would have never believed women knew such things."

163

"Pascal? I was just thinking about him. Imagining him playing." Hearing the name on his lips, she pulled him towards her. "You say he's safe. No, I'm not asking where. Just when …"

"Don't say *when*. Not like that. We'll spoil things if we start lying to each other. We both know what we're in for. I just can't forgive myself dragging you to this hell-hole. I'll die with that regret."

"You didn't drag me anywhere. I found you. Do you realise that poor woman had to fall for me to find you …?"

"Sylvie? You shouldn't think like that. You know she didn't fall. I'll tell you about it. We'd been sent to unpack clocks and toys that day. Sometimes the vans brought too many crates for the men. I remember Sylvie was on a table at the other end of the room. Brunner himself turned up that morning. They'd got us kitted out in clean aprons for the visitation but Sylvie missed out somehow. She was wearing this odd sort of gypsy skirt – red and black, very pretty. She's not much more than a girl."

She reached out, fumbling in his pocket for his cigarette case. Alex pulled it out, lighting a cigarette for her, her face flaring yellow in the flame. He waited, watching the glowing tip pulse red.

"Herr Brunner came sauntering over to my table. Stood there eyeing me up and down like a prize cow. He was all got up in his shiny uniform, smirking. You're supposed to stand to attention for an inspection, turning your head so you're always looking at whoever. He was tormenting us, striding up and down, flipping at a pile of pillow cases with his little cane. Suddenly there was this dreadful scream from the other end of the room. It was Sylvie. I remember thinking, why's he not looking. This expression on his face, as if he suddenly couldn't wait to get out."

"There were guards there? There must have been."

"Oh, yes, they were there. They were watching Sylvie. She walked into the middle of the room with this toy train in her hand. A big clumsy wooden thing. Home made."

"Oh, Christ, no …"

"She was shouting, *my God, my God, it's Paul's, it's little Paul's.* I'll die remembering that voice. Cracked, like it wouldn't work properly, like she'd never get it to work again. Then she sat down on the floor shoving the train back and forth in the rubbish, moaning to herself. Brunner was still there. We were all looking at him. That's what we had to do. He started shouting for the foreman, whacking at the piles of linen telling us to stop staring at him. But I couldn't. I just went on and on looking. It was like my eyes seemed to burn something on his face. Just for a second, before he walked away, there was this look ..."

"I know. I saw it somewhere this afternoon. Frightened. That's what you're going to say, isn't it?"

"After he'd gone, they brought the morning break forward on account of Sylvie. To calm us down, I suppose. There's a big flat roof up there. If it's not raining they let you walk about for a bit of fresh air. Sylvie came up with us. Nobody wanted to go near her, not even the guards. The poor woman walked up and down clutching her train, looking as if she was dead already. There were just the two guards that day, those strange yellow blokes that can hardly speak French. Sylvie went over to one of them and gave him the train. Then she straightened her skirt, gave an odd little smile and walked away. You wouldn't have wanted to stop her, Alex."

# twenty

A LEX could only guess how long she had been asleep, her head pressed hard against his shoulder, one hand enclosing his in some desperate gesture of possession.

She woke, drawing him closer, as he fumbled in his pocket for cigarettes, wearily staring into the darkness, conscious of sleeping bodies around them.

"What's the matter, love? You should sleep."

"Justine, listen."

She seemed to sense the tension in his voice, hauling herself up. "It's nothing. Just night noises in the building. It's always like this."

"No, about tomorrow. We have to plan while we can. Tell me what happens. As much detail as you can."

He felt the sag of her body as she pulled away.

"All that's a fantasy, Alex. Don't even think about it. If we start anything, they'll shoot all of us. I know this place."

"Those two ancient Russians? I doubt they can do much shooting."

"There are German soldiers downstairs. They'll be in charge of transport to Drancy. Soldiers everywhere. A few enjoy themselves mauling the women onto the bus but the others always stay well

166

back. Spaced along the back wall in the yard. They all have MP40s. There's a Bren gun in the yard. They're willing to take their own men down, if that's what's in your mind. Somebody made a run for it a few months ago and some poor corporal got in the way. We were worked nearly to death for that."

"No, not the loading – inside the bus, that will be the weak point. Think …"

"I've only been on the bus twice. There were armed guards. Two, I think. They stand on the conductor's platform at the back. Can you imagine a submachine gun in a bus?"

"When we get to Drancy?"

"If that's where they're taking us. Every time I've been, the bus didn't stop until it was inside the gates. The place is crawling with the Gendarmerie …"

"What d'you mean, *if*?"

"You heard what Cecile said. If they wanted to check our papers, why aren't they pestering us? You can see for yourself, nobody seems interested. She's right - Brunner has us lined up for his damned convoy. Rest on me a bit, Alex. Try to sleep. I'm going to sit quiet for a while."


He slept eventually, slumped against her body, conscious of the swell of her breast. A shallow restless sleep filled with a lucid dream.

He was a boy again, consumed with familiar fear, his face pressed to the cold glass of his bedroom windowpane. Looking down on the angled stones of the Lévitan store. Light so bright it burnt his eyes, Mother prodding him to say the doctor had come to cure his thirst. Clinging to sleep among a clank of buckets, Mother pulling him back into the consoling dark, relentlessly prodding him, Doctor Clérambault's thick catarrhal cough strangely synchronised with her hand.

He woke to a fierce thirst, a dreadful bitter taste in his mouth, his tongue shrivelled. A blaze of light cut lines through the thick blue haze of smoke.

167

Everywhere, a vague disordered whisper: the sound of fear.

Everywhere, the smell of raw shit.

Cecile was standing over him wriggling her shoe insistently into his back.

"Hell, you sleep like the dead. Here, I've found us something to drink."

She pressed a tin into his hand, the label bright yellow, two children beaming between slanted English words: *Pineapple Chunks.*

"Go on, have as much as you like, I have another. They were in one of the crates. Some poor soul must have been hoarding them."

"Justine?" He kneeled up, aware of a sudden pain in his side, staring in panic round the room. "Justine?"

"Over at the buckets. Best not to ask. Here, drink some. It's too sweet, but better than nothing. Don't look so tragic, the poor woman won't be long. God, this place stinks. Here's the other can."

She held out a long bolster-case, weighted down with the tin. "You'll have to help me with it. I'll have to hide it or they'll accuse me of theft. You soon learn they have a sense of humour, our German friends. I'm going to hide it under my dress somehow. I'm fat enough. And yes I have something to open it with. Can you help?"

"I've a belt … we might do something with that ... I'm not sure. I'm sorry, I'm barely awake."

"I can't take your belt. See whether you can find something over there. A piece of cord, that would do."

But Justine was already pushing him aside. "Cord? I know where there's some … let me."

Alex looked at Cecile. "Won't there be something to drink when we get there? At Drancy?"

She looked at him, knotting the pillowcase round her waist, her expression bleak. "*Drancy*? That what you think? I've been wondering why that maniac Brunner isn't interested in our papers any more."

168

She rose up on tiptoes, starting to count heads, abandoning the effort, exasperated. "How many are we? Forty? Fifty? That's a bus load. Enough to fill his last damned convoy. No, we're to be number seventy-seven, alright. Sounds lucky, doesn't it? We're for the station at Austerlitz, you see. That's why they didn't bother with water. Why should they? We're dead already. For God's sake, do I have to write it all down?" He could smell the acid pineapple on her breath, something dead in her eyes. "All I know is they won't be loading me."

She took a few steps, an awkward stumbling walk, swinging her weighted skirt. "Don't worry. I bequeath you my tin. You can have it when the time comes. I'm going to run for it when they try to get us on the bus. There's always a muddle then. What? You think I'm a bit old for running? A bit fat?"

"No … no, it's not that …" Alex was embarrassed, flailing, "but that's precisely when it's impossible. Look, we know about these things. Just accept we both know. If there's a chance, we'll help you take it, but you can't take chances with armed soldiers."

Seeing her start to shake her head, he pressed on, "You won't get more than a yard. They'll shoot you."

Cecile hitched the load up round her waist, facing him, her mouth set. "Don't take me for a fool, young man. I realise that perfectly well. I've realised it ever since they brought us back. One way or another, I'm afraid Herr Brunner's convoy will be leaving without me."

A door at the far end of the room rattled open. Not the door they had come in by, this was some kind of fire escape. A wave of warm musty air flooded into the room.

Two men in uniform stood in the doorway, looking in.

"Careful." Cecile was whispering in his ear. "*Kreiskommandanturen* – that's what they call themselves. Our resident German chums. The blond one is a sadistic devil."

He had walked into the room, prodding reluctant knots of people into a straggling line with the butt of a submachine gun. He seemed

169

harassed, sweat standing in beads on his forehead, endlessly pushing his cap back, sweeping locks of straw-coloured hair out of his eyes.

He stopped next to the buckets, retching violently, clearing his throat, spitting. The man in the doorway called him back, shaking the bolt of a rifle over a woman sitting on the floor.


A quiet voice, surprisingly gentle, counted them out as they filed past the guards onto a steep flight of concrete steps lit by a single electric bulb.

Alex supported Cecile, his back scraping the wall in a cramped space barely wide enough for two, people behind bearing down. At the half turn they could go no further, a solid wedge of bodies unbearably compressed against double doors closed with a metal bar. A woman somewhere far above lost her footing, a wave of sweating flesh rippling down.

Cecile began to swear, a steady stream of obscenities, her face purple, fighting for air.

The woman higher up the stairs was calling now, adding to the bedlam, shouting she could not breathe. Over and over again, an hysterical sing-song repetition, conjuring herself into madness.

The guard shouted for her to shut up, unexpected French silencing her for a moment, only for her wails to resume in another key.

*Stop it or I'll stop you.* The other guard stopped laughing, bellowing over their heads. *It'll be worse on the train. Die Tür! We can't stay here all day."*

Barely able to move, Alex wriggled his hand out pressing the iron rail, feeling solid wood resist. It swung free, grating across a concrete apron outside.

They were staring into the soft pink air of a Paris dawn.


A flood of people poured past, carrying him through the narrow door into a walled courtyard.

As the guard closed the door, an old man hung on, scrambling back inside. The guard leaned over, swinging the butt of his rifle with one hand. No more than a nonchalant tap, the gesture something to check an errant child, barely worth the effort. The blow caught the old man on the back of his neck pitching him face down on the ground. A woman at his side bent to lift him a little, abandoning the effort as the guard prodded her to re-join the others.

They stood in a mutinous circle round the door, muttering as the crumpled tortoise body shuffled itself backwards to lie unattended on the concrete.

Alex looked up to a patch of watery blue sky trying to get his bearings. They were at the foot of one of the ramps running down to the back of the shop, a massive circle of ribbed metal for turning the lorries filling most of a tiny courtyard.

Cecile walked across to the line of men standing against the far wall, reaching out, pressing her open hand against a bayonet, taunting the grinning soldiers manning the Bren gun.

Justine pulled her back. "Not here. Wait."

She tried to pull away, the whisper venomous, "I've told you. When the bus comes ... you'll see."

Alex stood alongside, taking her arm, pressing her tight between them. "You'll get a bayonet in your back. Now's not the time. You saw what they did to that poor devil."

He felt her shoulders fall, realising the truth of the matter. She had no intention of running. None of them had. When it came to it, courage was not enough. The night had taken something away from all of them. Fantasies of escape were all they had left. Imperceptibly, they had taken on their new identity, standing patiently in the pale sunlight like cattle, dimly conscious of their fate, vaguely restless.

Cecile faced him down, re-living some long forgotten piece of theatre, eyebrows framing a question he knew he could not answer.

She sighed heavily, "Perhaps you're right. Wait for better times."

"Here's the bus!"

Painted in shabby green, there was something affecting about this relic of another age warily negotiating the steep slope. Someone had wound the windows down for the summer weather.

It stopped at the foot of the ramp bringing the bitter smell of half-burnt oil into the courtyard. The driver climbed down, walking towards the guards.

"Where did that thing come from?" They were managing in a sort of French, "A museum?"

"There's a strike on." The driver seemed offended. "You're lucky they let me come. It's no picnic backing this thing down there."

He pulled a sheaf of papers from his pocket. "I'm to give you this. It's the bill. How many to take?"

"Forty-one. They said forty, but we're one over. She'll manage the extra will she? Not too heavy?"

The driver looked nervously at the Bren gun. "You're not bringing that thing on?" He flinched as one of the soldiers pivoted the barrel, noisily cocking the bolt, calling out, *Boom!*

"Not that thing on my bus. There's no room."

"No grandpa, just me on your bus." Poking the barrel of his MP40 into the driver's face, "And my friend here."

He shouted to the soldiers slouching against the wall. "You lot going to stand there all morning? Get these bastards loaded." Swivelling round on his heel, facing the crowd, "Move, you lot."

Men stepped aside in a pantomime of absurd courtesies, letting the women stumble forward first, holding on to each other, unsuitable shoes slipping on the ribbed surface of the metal circle.

They clambered onto their bus, neatly one by one, scuttling forward to settle on seats, as if compliance, even now, might ward off something worse.

172

# twenty-one

Alex was the last to board, standing alongside while Justine pulled Cecile onto a seat, leaning across her, penning her against him.

The guard swung onto the platform as the bus moved off, yanking at the bell cord to mocking cheers from the soldiers in the yard.

He gestured Alex to the empty seat across the aisle from Cecile, their eyes locking in a fleeting exchange. Alex stayed where he was, hanging onto the chrome rail next to where she sat. The guard looked away, conscious he had conceded something, bracing himself, legs apart, the MP40 cradled loose across his arms.

They were running fast down to the river, morning sun giving the empty streets a pastoral air, softening the stonework. A couple arguing on the corner stopped to watch their progress - elderly tourists staring mutely back.

Alex bent over Cecile's head stooping to see through the window. They were in the old Jewish quarter, rattling past the deserted cobbles of the rue Gravilliers. He had stood in that street, when was it? It seemed a lifetime ago.

"He's turning down to the river." Cecile pulled at Alex's jacket, looking up at him, her voice drowning in a ripple of panic spreading down the bus.

"This is the Boulevard de Magenta. It's the wrong way. Now d'you believe me?"

She grabbed hold of his shoulder, pulling herself up, standing next to him, her breath warm against his ear.

"This is the way to Austerlitz. That's where they're taking us. To the *Gare*."

She freed the heavy pillowcase from under her skirt, pressing the twisted linen into his hand.

"Here's the tin. I'll leave it for you two. Something to drink. They'll not get me in one of those trains." Pushing him aside. "Now, for God's sake, let me past."

Seeing her move, the guard rose awkwardly on tiptoes, straining to see.

"Let me go!" Her voice too loud, hoarse with the effort. "I have to get off."

Justine leaned across the seat pulling her back, Cecile feebly resisting, wrapping both arms round Alex's shoulders, her face smeared with tears.

"Tell her to leave me be. Christ in heaven, what have I done to come to this?"

At the bus stop on the corner a woman stepped into the road, signalling. The driver hesitated, veering over, the guard bellowing down the bus, *Drive on you bloody fool. We're not taking passengers!*

Cecile stood swaying in the aisle, reaching up to the leather pull cord above her head. Hearing the bell strike as she pulled it, she pulled again and again in a demonic frenzy, the noise drowning the guard's voice, *Drive on man, God damn you, drive on!*

The guard left the platform, shoving past Alex, swaying to keep his balance, transferring the gun to his left hand, standing hard against Cecile, the barrel pressed into her breast.

"I ask once. Sit down, old woman." Broken French menacingly calm, "Leave that alone."

Cecile let go of the pull cord, seizing the barrel with both hands, pulling him close, almost an embrace, both staggering back as the bus careered into the kerb, braking hard.

The guard reached out, grabbing her hair to keep his balance, yanking it hard. For a moment as he fell back onto a seat a puzzled expression crossed his face, his hand coming away filled with the soft mass of Cecile's curls. She cried out, the sound like some tiny injured bird, covering her ears, the dome of her bare scalp rising between her hands, a few straggled tufts of dark hair across her head glistening with sweat.

The bus had stopped, bouncing slightly with the pant of the engine.

The guard laid the MP40 on the seat at his side, sweeping the pile of hair to the floor, slowly unbuttoning the holster at his side. He drew the pistol out, turning it slowly in his hand as if trying to recall some detail of its operation.

Justine began sliding across her seat, reaching down to the slatted wooden floor to rescue the wig.

The guard kicked it away, motioning for her to stand next to Cecile.

"Go then." Leaning forward, his face set, waving his gun towards the conductor's platform. "Go."

Cecile walked slowly past him, pausing to push Justine down into her seat.

"No. Both of you. Go."

He turned slightly in his seat watching them pass, pulling the slide of the pistol back, cocking it. He stayed sitting where he was, the pose almost nonchalant, as if the task barely merited the effort to stand.

Justine had reached the platform, her arm round Cecile's shoulder. As she leaned slightly forward, the gun barrel dipped, echoing her movement, waiting for her to rise.

Alex swung the weighted pillowcase round. Heavier than he expected, the weight almost defeating him, coming in from the side, landing low. A merciless blow, the edge of the tin took the startled guard full in the face. His mouth opened, silently expelling air. Like some unimaginable conjuring trick, a cavity appeared in his cheek, an atrocious concave wound, spouting blood. The gun exploded in his hand a single bullet striking the roof.

The second blow splayed the soldier's cap across his skull, felling him like a poleaxed beast. Blind with rage, Alex tugged to strike again, the tin caught stubbornly in the polished metal of his cap badge, a patch of blood, too much blood, spreading through the fabric of the pillowcase.

Behind him, a tall theatrical figure had eased himself tentatively out of his seat. An old man, making the best of his rumpled state, bow-tie not quite straight. He made his quiet way to the conductor's platform almost apologetically, turning to look back down the bus, eyebrows raised, waiting.

An exodus had begun: passengers hurrying silently past the sleeping body, jumping down into the morning air.

Cecile walked back, rescuing the wig from the floor, standing for a second alongside Justine, squeezing her arm. They watched her waddle uncertainly into a disturbed ants' nest of aimless forms drifting around the stranded bus, slowly dispersing into the maze of side streets.

Alex panicked. "Justine, the driver. Stop him!"

"No driver." Her voice calm against the silence in the bus. "He's gone. Made a run for it. Cecile as well – we'll not see her again. They've all gone."

She walked down to see to the injured guard, stooping to prop him against the rail behind his seat, forcing his arms to support his body like some monstrous puppet. His mouth hung open, a thin clear liquid dribbling into it from one nostril. A mass of purple tissue spreading from the smashed cheek had sealed his right eye. As she let it go, his head banged hard against the rail.

"He's barely breathing. I think he's dying."

"He was going to shoot. I watched him cock the damned thing." Alex realised his hands were trembling. "What else could I do?"

"Nothing, nothing at all ... you saved my life."

She picked the submachine gun up, prising the pistol from the soldier's hand, handing them both to Alex. "We'll risk taking these with us. Let's hope we don't need them. I'm not sure where we are. Not that far from the river, I think. It will be the hell of a walk. But it's still early ... Alex, are you listening? You look terrible."

"He was scared, Justine. I saw it in his eyes when we first got on. I think he realised as soon as the bus started. There were too many of us for safety. He was frightened."

"What are you saying? You can't kill a frightened man? It was him or me. Perhaps there are honourable soldiers, I suppose there must be, but this man wasn't." She stood, pulling Alex up with her, leaning very close, her eyes hot with pain.

"Whenever you say we were the lucky ones, the ones who got away, remember those who didn't get away. Killed for their name on a bit of paper. Killed for existing. None of it has anything to do with war, none of it at all. Do you understand?"

She turned away from him, "Now we'd better get out of this."

As she made for the platform at the back of the bus, Alex called to her. He was standing next to the driver's battered leather seat, his expression something almost a smile.

"It can't be harder than a jeep. If I can see how you get the thing started."


They abandoned the bus on the Faubourg Saint Honoré where another platane lay across the road, the air filled with the scent of newly sawn wood. A makeshift barricade of paving stones had been piled behind the tree. Strips of asphalt lay about like immense rolls of black carpet.

A single rifle shot from an upstairs window echoed into the silence, answered by the stuttering chatter of an automatic weapon somewhere to their right, filling the street with the stretched metallic whine of ricocheting bullets.

Fifty yards beyond the barricade, two German soldiers were crouched inside the pockmarked portico of an apartment block. One of them raised a hand to Alex, almost a greeting, ostentatiously sending his carbine clattering into the gutter. Perhaps he called out – it was too far away to be sure.

The soldier wriggled on his stomach out of the tiny stone cage, his arms outstretched in an absurd gesture of surrender. He looked like a drowning child. He rolled back, screaming, as a single shot turned one extended hand to a sudden splash of red. They lay curled together against the stone steps like two children.

The firing stopped, an uncanny silence falling over the street. Not so far away, the sound of running feet, men's voices shouting, the smash of broken glass.

On the top floor of the apartment opposite somebody was furiously cranking a gramophone, pushing the mahogany box out onto a window-sill. The faint rickety sound of the *Marseillaise* floated into the street.

It seemed somehow unused to the open air.


It took an hour to find a way to Madeleine's apartment.

All that was left of the elegant glass doors to the street was a mosaic of splintered glass and wrought iron spread over the pavement. They picked their way through debris, broken glass grinding underfoot.

The metal lattice of the lift cage had been wrenched away, the tiny cabin inside draped with a frayed trade union banner, its circular medallion the hammer and sickle.

A trail of cigarette-ends led to the turn of the stairs on the second floor. A discarded army boot, thick with fresh blood, lay at the head of the marble stairs.

Madeleine's door was open wide, a haze of brownish smoke drifting out, the sweet acetone smell of gunfire.

Alex looked inside. In un-shuttered sunlight the paintings in the empty hallway seemed oddly unfamiliar. Broken pieces of the Chinese vase lay scattered among fallen faded flowers. He bent down, lifting a piece of hollow pottery, puzzled it should have lain unattended for so long.

It seemed months ago.


Down the corridor an excited chatter of men's voices suddenly stopped, the tiny frisson of silence broken by a single rifle shot, the sound too large for the space.

The salon door burst open. Madeleine stood frozen, staring at them, one hand clutching her breast.

"Dear Jesus - you here! I knew I'd never see you again. Either of you."

She started towards them, suddenly halting, looking beyond them into the hall, her eyes wild with sudden panic. "You're alone? God, yes ... of course ... on your own ... it's a miracle." Wrapping her arms round Justine, looking into her face, smudging tears away.

"We talked about you this morning ... well, dawn it must have been." She waved vaguely down the corridor. "My new tenants. Temporary, I hope. About rescue. Nonsense, of course, that Drancy place is a fortress. They were just trying to keep my spirits up."

She reared her head back, catching Justine off guard, shrewd eyes suddenly too inquisitive.

"And Drancy? They let you go? Has the fighting started there as well? Is that why? It started here this morning in the street. Men running everywhere. The police as well, they joined in. I heard a gang break in downstairs, rushing up the stairs, banging on the door

179

like savages. I thought they would kill me for sure. But it was just a bunch of students. Communists - you have to be young to say that. They wanted my balcony to shoot from. Then we decided the studio window was better. They've been in there ever since. The mess is incredible. One rifle between the lot of us … to save Paris! I've told them it's a start - God will manage the end."

She released Justine, instantly changing her mind, spreading her arms round the two of them, pulling them close, tears running down her face, managing a choking sort of laugh.

"They've started treating me like their mother. It was a mistake making them food - they've been here ever since. I came to get them something to drink. Come with me, I want to keep you where I can see you. I still can't believe you're here."

In the kitchen, the window looked across a narrow lane to the backs of another apartment block. The noise was louder, an incessant chatter of automatic weapons rattling the china on the dresser. There seemed to be no target – the tiny alleyway was deserted.

Madeleine uncorked a bottle of wine, rushing out, leaving them eyeing each other like unexpected visitors, neither daring to speak.

In the alley below, a lorry was inching towards a barricade, low gears screaming, soldiers in the open back peering over an improvised palisade of slatted wood. One steadied his rifle on the cab, aiming high, tottering back as the lorry began to turn, clumsily shunting between the narrow pavements.

Alex flinched as something dark cartwheeled past the window. A bottle burst on the road, spraying liquid under the lorry. A second bottle landed inside the wooden pen, spinning round, unbroken. The soldiers kicked it away looking up into a hail of bottles. There were bottles everywhere now, too many to count, the lorry standing on a carpet of green glass.

The soldiers in their wooden pen knew long before the smell reached the kitchen. Heaving themselves in panic over the sides, clambering into the mess of shattered glass, ineffectual arms covering their heads, grey shapes scuttling from one impossible shelter to the next. The kitchen reeked of the stuff now - petrol everywhere, fresh and raw on the air.

The bottles stopped. For a frozen second nothing moved, the men staring blindly round dizzy in the heady scent.

Something small, feather-white, floated down, twisting innocently to the ground, the street blooming into a mass of yellow flame.

Pygmy forms, alight like torches, filled the street, fleeing one another, each a screaming vortex of flame, collapsing into writhing mounds of smouldering cloth.

Alex felt his gorge rise. "God almighty. That smell …"

Justine stared blindly into the smoke, finally taking his hand, pulling him away. She was trembling.

"I didn't realise. Paris has been a pretence, hasn't it, Alex? All that kept me alive was thinking I'd see Pascal again. But we won't, will we? Not now the war has arrived. We're not going to get away, are we? We're still trapped."


It was a long time before Madeleine came back. She had a young man with her, his face flushed with the excitement of unaccustomed power. He held out a hand to Alex then seeing it was black with oil pulled back, offering the sleeve of his overall, a peasant gesture, oddly touching.

"He wants me to go and talk to someone – I have to go out."

Hearing Madeleine speaking English, the boy glanced at Alex, unaccountably embarrassed.

"It seems they've taken a prisoner. Apparently not a soldier, but throwing his weight about in three languages. I think they want somebody to adjudicate. The man had my name and this address – and that's a mystery." She turned to Alex.

"Will you come with me? I have no idea what it's about."

"Out in the street? They took our papers."

"Then best you stay here. He can't eat me, whoever he is."

The boy became impatient, addressing Alex in French. "He's asking to see the Colonel."

He watched Madeleine's expression change, hardening. "What's he talking about? *Colonel?* Are there troops here?"

Madeleine pulled him to one side, throwing a smile at the boy, whispering. "He understands more English than you think. It's no use asking that question. They've organised themselves like the military … ranks, titles ... and so forth. They all have arm bands. I suppose there has to be a hierarchy. You find it all juvenile?"

"No. I find it impressive, but you can't fight a war with armbands. Do they know what's in store when the garrison turns out?"

Another shot exploded at the end of the corridor, the first in minutes. Startled, Madeleine took the boy's arm, giving Alex a brief Gallic shrug.

"You won't stop them now. You saw that business with the lorry? It's too late to stop. Too late. Now … where are you taking me young man? Not far, I hope."

"You know the bar. The *Leopard.* We have to go out the back way."


They watched them through the kitchen window, arm in arm, stepping gingerly through scattered broken glass. The street was ominously silent, the burnt-out lorry now part of the barricade. A plume of oily black smoke drifted languidly from one smouldering tyre.

In the street beyond, tricolour flags sprouted impudently from the higher windows.

On the corner, Madeleine paused for a second, turning to look back, steadying herself on the boy's arm. They walked out of sight.

Looking down, a nun with a tiny makeshift flag tied to a walking stick shuffled out from a doorway, the huge wings of her headpiece flapping white. Two men with a stretcher scuttled in her wake, bodies bent double against imaginary gunfire.

They stood next to the soldier in the middle of the road. He had curled up like a sleeping child, unbearably still.

## twenty-two

A Matisse hung on the wall opposite the empty fireplace in Madeleine's salon. Perhaps not a masterpiece, but her proudest possession. Alex could not remember a time when the reclining woman in red pyjamas had not been hanging in this room. She lay against a sombre pattern of red and blue, her face no more than a few bleak dabs of black, one arm raised to touch her forehead as if warding something off.

For reasons they dared not acknowledge they had left the door to the apartment open to the vague menace beyond the hallway outside, sitting together silent on the large sofa waiting for Madeleine to return, letting darkness consume the painted odalisque.

Outside, the revolution – if that was what it was - had contracted to no more than unfamiliar footsteps on the stairs, voices calling in the dark, now and then the sound of shattering glass.

It was late when she returned, hurrying feet across the tiled hallway taking them by surprise. She hesitated for a moment at the door, perhaps puzzled that it was still open.

*No, this is far enough. Goodnight.* A man's voice, faintly from the floor below, Madeleine calling back, conceding something.

She was still smiling when she found them in the salon, dropping her coat onto a chair.

"Sitting in the dark. I used to do that. But they say the blackout is ending. They say that. Shall we see? Go on, Alexandre, switch them all on."

She let him take her arm, steadying herself against him, her breath warm on his cheek.

"There, I can see you now. I'm afraid I'm a little drunk. They opened champagne to celebrate something. Being alive, I assume. They insisted I drink with them. After all, it was not their champagne."

She flopped onto the sofa, looking up at Alex. "Well, it seems it has begun. A very Parisian war, with breaks for refreshment. And don't the soldiers come young! Here, sit by me, I feel a little light-headed – expansive you might say. I have a story to tell. Alex, bring a chair, sit close where I can hear you. Then we will eat ... how I miss my Stephanie."

Justine sat next to her on the sofa. "Your mysterious man in need of adjudication – you saw him?"

Madeleine leaned back, one hand pressed to her eyes, against the electric light. She seemed to have aged since she went away: tiny spots of feverish red on her cheeks, a kind of slackening of the skin around her mouth.

She sighed, as if speech would, after all, be too great an effort.

"*See him*? Yes, of course I saw him." Looking at Alex, searching for his eyes, waiting for him to return her gaze.

"But I heard him long before I saw him. Bellowing like a madman. Can people with squeaky voices bellow? The boys in the bar said he'd become tiresome, shouting like a bad-tempered schoolmaster. So they locked him in a storeroom upstairs. They asked me to stop him making such a noise."

She looked down at her hands, stretching them out in her lap, frowning slightly as if something about them was displeasing.

"That was where I found him. A plump little fellow, full of hurt dignity, sitting among the empty beer bottles. I must say, after today it was hard listening to hurt dignity, even in good French. And yes, I admit his French was good."

She seemed to be waiting for Alex to acknowledge something, something unfathomable in her expression, a kind of provoking smile.

"At least, good for an Englishman."

Alex stared back at her, aware of movement about his heart, his pulse rising.

"English? But he must have known you. He sent for you."

"I'd never seen him before in my life. But I guessed who he was even before they unlocked the door."

The smile was still there.

"He introduced himself, but shall I describe him? I said *plump*. Too kind really. *Fat* would be better. Quite short. Peering at me through his little spectacles. Ugly thick glass. Shiny face - *like a baby's bottom* as they used to say – his cheeks puffed out like an angry toad. When he saw they'd sent a woman visiting, he looked me up and down. I even got an insolent little bow, passing the inspection. I could have slapped his face."

Alex stood up, feeling a momentary dizziness, his heart oddly unloosed in his chest. He walked to the balcony doors, twitching the curtain aside, holding on.

She leaned back, calling to him, almost a provocation. "Where are you going, Alex? What do you think he said, this little English *bonhommne*? I wish I could imitate, it was really splendid - *I've so much wanted to meet you*. Oxford English, don't you say? I thought he was going to kiss my hand."

"What the devil are you trying to say? It was John Cabot. Is that what you're saying? My God, that man's not a joke. But he doesn't know you. I can't believe it's him."

"I'm afraid you will have to believe it, Alexandre." She seemed irritated, "And I can't see you if you stand there sulking. As for knowing me, apparently you are responsible for that. He explained that my address appears in your file. Do you really have a *file*?"

He came slowly back to his chair, slumping down, nodding wearily. "*A file*? Yes ... yes ... of course. I knew that was possible. That someone could go looking. I'm sorry to wish him on you."

"Perhaps you may not be so sorry after all. He has proved useful. You know, he was not at all what I expected, Alexandre, this evil Moriarty of yours. To be in the presence of the devil incarnate and what do I find? A pompous little man locked up in a storeroom. I'm afraid he saw the disappointment in my face ... well, there you are, I could never hide my thoughts. You can't mend a thing like that. So we got off to a bad start."

Justine took her hand, glancing across at Alex. "You don't know about him. He deceived Alex. Badly. I think that was why he was looking for him."

Alex was blinking at his watch, as if he barely believed it, rounding on Madeleine, suddenly remembering something.

"That young chap who came back with you? We heard him. Can I get to him? Can he take me? It's not that late."

"My escort? He was excusing himself. Not a very military excuse. He said he was late for his supper and his mother would be worried. You see, even communists have mothers."

She pushed herself up, wincing slightly, pressing her head into the cushion. "I have a headache. No, you are too late. Mr Cabot left long before I did. A long time ago ... a lot of champagne ago. Two men arrived in a car to collect him. Waving papers signed by General Gerow at us, as if we cared. They said they had to drive him back to Montlhéry tonight. I'm not sure where that is. Apparently there's been fighting there ... that was why they were late."

"*Gerow* - but he's American ..."

"American ... yes. I assume that is how they managed to come. Apparently it is not impossible to come and go ... a matter of payment. Mr Cabot works for them. No uniform, of course, but certainly American. You know the kind? A little too big for the room

- very clean, smelling of chewing gum. You can imagine the excitement in the bar. Our first Americans. Even without the helmets."

"*Works for them*? How can he be working for them ...?"

Madeleine impatiently tapped the side of the sofa, interrupting him, "There, I knew I'd forget. He asked particularly to be remembered to you. He said he was sure Captain Vere would recall. He had warm memories of a time you worked together. Is that right? You worked together?"

"Is this a joke? For heaven's sake - the man had me locked up."

"He told me he arranged for you to be posted to Scotland. Is that locked up?"

Justine made room as Madeleine stretched out, closing her eyes, as if from some secret pain, the posture a curious echo of the Matisse on the wall behind. Speech seemed almost too great an effort.

"He told me what you did in France. A little of what you did. What both of you did." She reached out, finding Justine's hand.

"I didn't know, I am ashamed. You are braver souls than me." Opening her eyes to look down at Justine's hand, patting it, as if confirming some shared secret.

"Alexandre - Mr Cabot is envious of you, did you know? Or perhaps *jealous* is better. English is so difficult." She managed a watery smile. "I would kiss you for it, but I am a little tired."

She pulled Justine closer, her voice low, "I knew your *Alex* when he was just a child. He was always a modest little boy. You can kiss him in my place. Look at him now, staring at me in that disagreeable way. Alexandre, your Cabot man bears you no ill will, I know that."

"I'm sorry, you can't possibly know that. He had me locked away. How much ill will is that?"

"For your own safety, he said. Too much would be lost if you were captured. Surely you know war cuts corners? If you had lived here these past few years ..." She shrugged, "War doesn't care about people. They just get in the way. Dear God, who am I to be explaining? Mr Cabot sent you a message. I am to tell you that his war has been at least as trying as yours. Life is too short to bear grudges, Alexandre. Don't you want to know my news?"

"I don't care what he did to me. All that's over. It's what he did to Justine …"

Justine came to him, kneeling alongside his chair, her back to Madeleine, whispering, "Alex, love, please don't. You mustn't jump to conclusions ... not about me."

She turned to Madeleine, trying for a bright voice. "Your news. He promises he'll be quiet. But you look awfully tired ... perhaps tomorrow …?"

"No, it's too important for that. Mr Cabot arrived with orders for our arrondissement. The boys had told him no one believed in those things any more ... orders, I mean. They wouldn't even let him read them out. And you can understand, because when he read them to me it was completely preposterous. Poor Mr Cabot … like a character in one of those sentimental American films that Stephanie adores. Americans believe such odd things about the French. I think it's because we don't speak English – it's seen as a kind of mental handicap."

She looked at Alex, "Now … if you promise not to interrupt me, I will tell you what Mr Cabot was doing while you were in Scotland. *Locked up* as you say. He was in the United States of America. Not locked up, I imagine."

Alex frowned at her, shaking his head, "No, no, no that doesn't make sense. I'm sorry, I'm not interrupting you. It's just wrong. He's lying. Look, you don't know him. His profession is lying. It was Cabot who tricked Justine into coming to Paris. He is responsible for all of it. It was his trademark trick. He couldn't have done that if he was in the States. It would be impossible."

Madeleine seemed barely to hear him, pressing on, her voice hoarse with the effort. "At a training school in Virginia. He has been there until he arrived in Normandy a few weeks ago. Why should he lie to *me* about such a thing? It has nothing to do with me. But surely

189

you can check if it matters that much. He said a place called Charlottesville. Do you know where that is?"

Alex sat staring down at the patterned wood of the floor, a kind of defeat closing him in, contradictory truths leaving him slightly sick.

"Charlottesville. Yes, there's an Officer Academy there. And yes, it's in Virginia." He summoned up one last desperate effort, his voice insistent, "But just because Cabot knows that, doesn't mean he was there. Disinformation is his speciality. It's a skill you can't export. Anyway, the Americans have their own tricks. There would be nothing sensible for him to do."

"His work had nothing to do with disinformation." Her sudden feeble laugh took them both by surprise, forcing a faint uncomprehending smile to Justine's lips. "Although, *misinformation* might do. He was training civilians to govern France. The Civil Authority – that is what he called it. Do you believe me now? It would be a curious thing to lie about. In fact, I know he is not lying. We have known about that nonsense for weeks."

"When you say *we*?"

"Well ..." She seemed to find the question embarrassing. "I thought I told you. People of the *Quartier*. We were told about this insane plan shortly after the invasion – after the *landings* as you call it. Americans going from town to town, claiming them in the name of Uncle Sam. Mr Cabot's pupils, one assumes. They have even printed us new money. French dollars, you could say."

"You mean dealing with the Vichy lot? Surely ... "

"I mean no such thing. Why should they care about that? I mean settling who shall govern France. The Americans have decided – after all, it is their victory. And the answer is *not France*. Mr Cabot brought a list of names."

Seeing Alex shaking his head, she turned to look at the Matisse, her voice rising. "You see it's impossible, don't you? Thanking God to be rid of Germans, finding you are to exchange them for Americans. American curfews must be much the same as German curfews. You still can't go anywhere. And he really imagined that, in Paris. I can tell you - people would rather die."

"People are dying already."

"You said he was very clever, Alexandre. Your Mr Cabot. He can't bear the thought that it has become a farce. People are laughing at him. He never imagined he'd be locked up with the empty bottles. I suppose that's why he poured his soul out to me. At least that way, he saved a little face. But, my God, he was so solemn, it was hard not to laugh. Kept saying, *you realise, Paris is doomed?*"

"But the man's got eyes ..." Absurdly, Alex found himself defending Cabot. "He can see for himself what's going on. You think a few angry students? You think it's going to end well? How can it?"

"You mean my young men? Infant communists Mr Cabot called them. It's odd - he says he doesn't believe in them. Not particularly rational for a clever man. He says the whole situation is unreal. That was his word – *unreal*."

"He means how insanely unequal it is – that's what makes it unreal. This uprising - how many are involved? A thousand? Two thousand? Most of them unarmed. The German garrison is twenty times that. Armed soldiers with tanks - there must be fifty tanks or more in the city. There are scores of half-tracks, mobile artillery, the lot. How are a few ancient rifles supposed to liberate Paris?"

"He said he found the word *liberate* unfortunate. He is careful with words, Mr Cabot. I must say, it was difficult to warm to him. Superior without anything particular to be superior about. Lecturing me about how France will be governed. I told him, we have had one military government. We are not looking for another. He's a fool."

"He's one of the brightest people I've known."

"Then you have led a very cloistered life, Alexandre. I told him to go and ask those students the Germans were shelling this afternoon. Near the Sorbonne. Ask them if they want some American who barely speaks French as their new Mayor. Do they want to take their city back, or live under some absurd *Pax Americana*? If it wasn't for the fact he could help me, I would have walked away."

"What help? Why should Cabot help anybody?"

"Ah, as to *why* I can only guess. He mentioned this painting you talk about. He seemed to think I understood. I told him we have to get you out of Paris. He has papers that allow passage at the Porte d'Italie. It cost him nothing to give me them. He was not at all unwilling. They are there in my coat."

Trying to sit up, she found the effort too much, falling back against the cushions.

"If you would pass ..." Her eyes had closed. Justine reached out, resting a hand on her knee.

"She's not well. I think she's fainted. She's dreadfully pale."

"It's hot in here. I'll get some water."

"No it's not the heat. Look." Something in Justine's voice made him turn.

"There's blood all over the cushion. God, we've been sitting here all this time and she's hurt. Her shoulder, I think. I'll see if I can lie her down. See what you can find in the bathroom. Hurry."

## twenty-three

ALEX carried Madeleine to her bedroom. She seemed unconscious, her eyes only flickering open as he laid her on the bed. Bending over her, he found mild blue eyes close to his own, a faint ironic smile wrinkling her face.

"Hell, when did I last look up at a man like this?"

She tried to lift herself, falling back, cursing. "I must have passed out. And where's this you've brought me?"

Justine began unbuttoning her dress, gently pulling it away at the shoulder. Madeleine pushed her off.

"Here, let me. I can manage. I remember now, I was feeling dizzy. I can't manage this button. Too feeble."

Justine leaned over to inspect the wound. "It's very raw. It looks like a bullet, but ..."

"Don't go hunting for bullets, you'll find nothing. The boys already looked. A graze, they said. Quite deep, but just a graze. I remember the damned thing felt like a knife. Why the long face, Alexandre? There are some dressings in the bathroom. Go and see what you can find. It's not the end of the world. They said it was nothing."

"What would they know?" Justine sounded angry. "Kids playing soldiers. It's been bleeding quite badly."

"There was a crowd outside in the road. Drunk, I think. Somebody shot through the door of the bar. Hit the wall. This thing was a ricochet. Unlucky."

The smile for Alex turned to a grimace, her teeth bared in pain.

"You may fetch the dressings then you may go away. I'm not an exhibition. Justine will deal with me. Go to bed, you look very tired. Don't use all the hot water. I made your room ready this morning – a little act of supplication. We will talk about it in the morning. I intend to be still alive."

She rolled painfully onto her side as he left the room, reaching a hand out to Justine, her face drawn.

"We'd better see what's to be done. A nuisance."


It was late when Alex finally climbed the narrow staircase to the floor above. He heard Justine laugh as he passed Madeleine's room, the two women talking over each other.

The scent of cedar wood on the staircase peeled away the years. How many times had he slept in the room at the end of this passageway? It must have been hundreds. His own little room, for surely no one else had ever slept there.

It had not changed: his homework desk still tucked between the two windows, the same tiny chairs parked on either side. Frail things, too delicate for sitting, upholstered in grey *toile de jouy*. Even the chamber pot beneath the bed.

The picture was still there, filling most of the only free wall. Hard to imagine it anywhere else: a clumsy painting of water lilies, the signature, *Claude Monet, 1919*, optimistic. He had asked her once why she bothered with such a bad copy, remembering only now that she had never replied.

The bed was freshly made, sheets turned back, a lace-edged bolster plumped against the wall behind. There was a pack of Sobranie Russian cigarettes on the little *chevet*. She had done all this today. Even the carafe of water with its scrap of beaded linen to keep the dust away. Futile rituals warding off the certainty she would never see him again, never see either of them ever again.

He woke to the sound of someone tapping at the door, suddenly bolt upright, flailing to find the electric cord, staring wildly at a figure silhouetted in the open doorway, barely knowing where he was.

"Oh, you're asleep. I startled you. Madeleine followed me to my bath. She wanted to talk."

"Madeleine, yes ... I'm sorry ... still half asleep. Is all well?"

"The wound is nothing much. She's very professional about such things. There's things you don't know about your aunt, Alex."

"I know she's involved in some sort of Home Guard effort. Perhaps it's become more than that now. Those bandages in the bathroom were French Army issue. Surgical dressings. Not for when you cut your finger."

Justine walked to the window, looking down into the road, her voice muffled against the dark of the windowpane. She seemed strangely defenceless.

"I left Madeleine in her own bed." Turning to face him, her expression defiant. "She said I am to impose on you. She thinks she's being kind. And don't look like that, it's not fair. It's a ridiculous thing to say, but I feel shy. Turn the light off – I'll manage perfectly well in the dark."

He felt the movement of the bed as she settled alongside him, immobile on her back, bringing with her the fresh perfume of Madeleine's soap.

"Can we talk a little, Guffin? I'm dreadfully tired, but it will make me feel less odd. About Cecile and that hideous man Brunner. Do you think she could have got away?"

Alex reached out finding her hand. "Yes, I'm sure of it. You're asking about us, aren't you?"

"I suppose so. It's all this madness starting. I'm thinking about him all the time. Perhaps I'll go mad."

"Pascal?" He felt her move at the name, turning towards him. "If what you're asking is should we trust Cabot and his papers, how can I answer? I've spent so long mistrusting that man. I seem to have lost my bearings."

"The Porte d'Italie. Is that far from here, do you know?"

"Not very. I suppose you could walk in an hour or two. Or one of those dog-cart things if they're not on strike. But we can't walk through a war. This business will start again tomorrow, probably worse. Then what? How long before the German garrison is on the streets?"

"Madeleine is sure the Germans have no intention of holding Paris. No, Alex, that's what she says. Give me your other hand. If you'd only heard her. She is convinced she's right."

"But all she knows is hysterical rumour. The city must be full of it. Cabot is right about that – it's unreal."

"She said the Germans in Paris have lost heart. Perhaps she knows. She lives here. She told me about these two soldiers penned up in a house on the rue du Jura. This was yesterday. There was a crowd outside, fifty or more, baying for their blood. They shot themselves. Can you believe that? Shot themselves, rather than come out with their hands up."

"Two soldiers against a mob ... yes, but ..."

"You're not seeing the point. Madeleine says it's like that everywhere. That's what Cabot didn't understand. It's not just a few thousand students, it's pretty well everybody now. Paris has fallen into a sort of madness. Nothing is going to stop it. If the Garrison starts a fight they will be torn to pieces whatever the cost, and they know it. It doesn't matter nobody's armed. People are mad with rage."

Feeling him about to speak, she pulled him very close. "You do know I'm right about this, my love ... think … this morning on that bus … with Cecile. You remember?"

She turned over, curling her back against his side. "It's lovely having you here. I've been out of the way of being held. Hold me,

Guffin, would you? We should sleep. I'll be here for you when you wake."

The air raid came before dawn, Alex swimming up into a blind confusion of sound, the drum of heavy engines, unbearably close. He sat up, searching for the window, a patch of lighter dark. Two planes. Or three in close formation. Hard to tell. Directly overhead now, engines whining in descent, the noise immense, unspeakably close.

Justine woke beside him, gripping his arm, flashes of yellow filling the room with obscure shadows, the sky above the city outside vaguely luminous.

The explosions rippled towards them like the slow tearing of wood, flexing the window glass.

It was finished before they had had time to move, engines straining in a steep climb. Towers of smoke reached up into a bloom of soft pink, low clouds shimmering alive.

"Is it over?" She was trembling, her voice unsteady, "They were ours, weren't they? I keep thinking how strange to be killed by our own bombs. Can you make out where they've gone? It seemed to be east. Perhaps they're not just bombing Paris. It did seem east, didn't it?"

"Not ours. Not American either. The engines weren't big enough. Heinkels, I think. That would explain no ack-ack. I think they were bombing the Marais. They were climbing away … probably just the one sortie. You're thinking of him, aren't you? They'll have shelters, surely …"

Justine got out of bed, standing at the window, her voice flat. "I suppose so. You can only see sky, Alex. Everywhere seems on fire. You wouldn't think a few bombs could do that. Whole streets alight …"

"One way of leaving little behind. Barely a trace, you'd say - not a rack. I start to think Madeleine's right. The Germans have decided to leave. Come back to bed, Justine."

"I won't be able to sleep. I'm not tired any more. What time is it?"

"I don't know. Very early."

He lit two cigarettes. They lay side by side watching the sky fade to the grey-pink of a Paris dawn.

Somewhere in the street below a single blackbird began its morning song.

"It will be the same for the store, won't it?" She had been silent for so long her voice startled him. "I mean for Lévitan and the other places? It will be exactly the same."

"The same how?"

"Erased. Forgotten. Not burned, just forgotten. Last night Madeleine said it would be like throwing letters in the fire. Things you don't want to read. An amnesic conspiracy she called it. The slave labour, the death camps, the endless misery, poor little Sylvie. All of them. It will all have gone."

"What do you think yesterday was about? If Paris survives ..."

"Oh, Paris will survive, Paris decided to look the other way a long time ago. Paris decided to find something else to do. I don't blame them ... misery piled on misery ... you reach a point when it's too much. Once you decide to forget, it's not so hard, you know ... not if you never quite believe in the first place. I'll never be able to explain. You have to have lived through it."

"That's why I will never forgive Cabot. If it wasn't for him, you wouldn't have had to live through it. Nothing would forgive him that."

"You don't have to forgive him, Alex. I don't believe he had anything to do with those men who came to Dundee, if that's what you think. I made a terrible mistake visiting Lucile Beyrou."

"What mistake? And if it wasn't Cabot, then who? The whole scheme has his fingerprints all over it."

"As for his fingerprint, yes perhaps, I can see that. I dare say whoever did it enjoyed tweaking his tail that way. Revenge you might say. Perhaps they thought it convenient for Mr Cabot to get the blame, but it wasn't him."

"Then who?"

"I don't know. D'you think I haven't worried myself sick as to who? Getting me back for killing Major Gliess – they don't forget things like that."

"Germans?"

"Or the Vichy lot - they had reasons. You realise, apart from those first men in Dundee, everybody I met was French? Don't you find that odd?"

"But how could it ever work? You'd resigned. You couldn't be sent on missions, fake or not - it doesn't make sense. I'm not likely to forget that day you came back from Baker Street? That day you resigned your commission."

"But it wasn't true, my love, it wasn't true. I saw you thought it … I saw you wanted to believe it. I hadn't the heart to explain … I just let you go on believing. When it came to it, I couldn't walk away. It's right, what they say about the Service - it's a sort of marriage. You're theirs for life."

"Why shouldn't you see this artist? Why's it a mistake? I saw her myself. She knows nothing at all. To tell the truth, I've never understood all the fuss about her. Never understood all that effort just to hide an obscure artist away. Nobody's heard of her."

"She's not obscure, Alex, not at all. And remember where she spent most of her life – our safe house. You just don't know her name. Madeleine knows her work. She's horribly famous. Sometimes when I think she actually painted my portrait …" She hesitated, "Alex, you're going to say I'm being mysterious. But I'm not. It's just hard for me to explain. About Lucy's picture …"

"You mean the one Cabot stole? What's there to explain?"

"He didn't steal it, he bought it – and thank God he did. You knew they put it on show? That painting was the mistake."

"What, because it almost has the same title as a Bradley painting? That's a bit far-fetched. Who's going to make that connection? Justine, what's this all about? Why the hell is everything always a secret?"

She suddenly sat up, reaching across him to switch on the light, her face wet with tears. "But you can know, Alex, of course you can know. I hate hearing you say things like that."

She gave him a little broken smile, searching for a handkerchief.

"You can have my little secret, my love. It's something Lucy explained. All those years she spent working with Bradley. They were very close. One day, he told her about the woman in that painting of his, the famous one, the one in the straw hat. She was my mother. That's all. That's my secret – nothing so very important. She died bringing me into the world. Spanish 'flu. It sent Bradley a bit mad. More than that – she said he was literally insane for a while. For years all he did was paint her. Dozens and dozens of paintings. He would finish them and burn them in the garden. Nobody had heard of him in those days. France was in ruins after the war. He was destitute, in and out of hospital. Perhaps he could have done something about me, but the truth is he didn't. I ended up handed over to nuns, just one more war baby. He never knew what became of me. I don't know, perhaps he never knew I existed."

"But if she was your mother …"

She smiled at him, shaking the hair out of her eyes, "Albert Bradley was my father. There you are … not so much of a secret."

"And her painting of you?"

"I suppose she was reaching out to me, picking that title. *Fille au Chapeau de Paille*. Of course, the word is *daughter*, not *girl*. That's what made it so dangerous."

She lay silent for a long time. "That's what brought those men to Dundee, whoever they were. It wouldn't be so hard to put two and two together. Cabot had nothing to do with it. In fact, you could say he did what he could to mend it. Too late, of course. You realise I was propped up in a London gallery window for weeks. She'd even signed the damned thing. She might as well have titled it *Portrait of an Agent* and included a map to the safe house."

# twenty-four

THE sound of rain pattering against the open window woke him, a fresh damp scent blowing past fluttering curtains. Justine's side of the bed was empty, her bedclothes thrown back. Alex stretched out one arm, paddling the cool sheets where she had lain, aware of an inexplicable feeling of contentment.

Madeleine was standing at his bedside.

"I've been watching you. You sleep like a little boy. Here, I've brought you your chocolate. A small cup, I'm afraid. All I've been permitted to carry. I've one good hand at least."

"Yes, your shoulder. I remember." He struggled to sit up. "You look better - quite cheerful, in fact. Have you seen Justine?"

She placed the tiny cup and saucer on the *chevet* at his bedside.

"Justine? Up and about long ago." She looked wistfully at his little homework desk. "I remember you sitting there. Would you believe I was weeping in here not so long ago? I'd found some cigarettes for you. Cigarettes you would never smoke. There I was weeping for your lost princess. I was sure I'd never see you again. When she came down this morning she started weeping herself. No, Alexandre, calm yourself, tears of quite another kind."

"I overslept. D'you know what time it is? Where is she?"

"Making the Colonel his breakfast. Stephanie was helping, so I ran away. I can't bear too many people in a kitchen."

"*Colonel*? You mean he's actually here? Is this about the raid? I thought I heard shooting earlier ... but a long way away."

"He came with my friend from the *Leopard*. Your Mr Cabot. The Americans turned him back."

"Cabot here? And this Colonel – what's he want?" Scrabbling for the kitbag lying on the floor next to the bed, "If it's papers ... is it that?"

"Heavens, no! Not papers. Leave them where they are. He showed no interest at all in papers." She smiled benevolently down. "I'd say he was more interested in the three women in the kitchen. That's at least two too many. I'll let you get dressed. Now drink up before the day runs away: your grandmother used to say that. I'm going in search of milk and bread. I will try the *Leopard* – you never know."

As she reached the bedroom door she seemed suddenly to remember something, turning to face him. "I forgot. Stephanie said she was taking your German guns. The things you brought with you. You are famous, by the way, both of you. People make pilgrimages to your abandoned bus. It's become a sort of shrine."

"There was a German soldier ... we had to leave him behind. Do you know ...?"

"Your chocolate is getting cold. I remember you used to call it *cocoa* when you were a little boy."

She walked across to collect the cup, hovering over him, reluctant to leave.

"Strange to be visiting little Alexandre's room. I could never bring myself to change the furniture. Another shrine, I suppose." She nodded to the vast canvas on the wall. "Even that Monet. Tucked away up here. Nobody ever sees the thing."

She began twisting the cup in her hand, lost for how to broach something, nerving herself up. "It was always compromised, you know, the pleasure I took in having you here. Always a little compromised."

"I wouldn't worry - kids imagine they're important, the centre of the world. Demanding little devils. I don't think I've changed all that much, to tell you the truth. I suppose I was always getting under your feet. Funny though - I always thought of myself as an obedient little chap."

"*Obedient*? Yes, I believe so. I am explaining badly. What I mean is I envied my sister her little boy. Jealousy - that was the compromise. Playing at mothers is a very seductive game, a sort of drug. And now you're going to say, *Why not one of your own? Why not a little boy of your own?*" She shrugged, trying to smile, "Perhaps the day will come I tell Justine that story. I like talking to your princess."

She posed herself on the edge of the bed, resting one hand lightly on his arm, her face taut with an odd intense expression. "The truth is I dislike responsibility. I prefer borrowing to owning. Perhaps you find that shameful?"

Alex stretched out for his cigarette case, smiling to himself as she avoided his eyes.

"If I didn't know better, I would say my beloved aunt is being *adept*. Heaven knows where you learned that trick. There's really no call to steer me, you know. I'm only too willing to talk about him. About another little boy, that is. It's just that I daren't. Not yet. You know, Justine said she had to ration thinking about him. It's too much like tempting fate. He's safe, that's all I know. She says he's safe. That's her rock and she's clinging to it. I realised last night, perhaps he's closer than I'd imagined. That raid upset her dreadfully. She asked me where the bombers were going next."

"Being responsible for someone like that ... it's unbearable. That's the difference between owning and borrowing. You really don't know where he is? And now I feel guilty. She told me yesterday. She told me everything."

"I'm the one person she won't tell. She wants us to find him together. I think I understand."

Madeleine squeezed his arm, easing herself up, gathering his cup. She had pulled a handkerchief from her sleeve, bunching it tight into her other hand waving vaguely to the window. "Look, the rain has stopped. Do you think that means our little war will start again? Come down when you're ready. Breakfast is in the kitchen. You will find your Mr Cabot there."

He looked up, puzzled by the tremor in her voice. There were tears in her eyes.

The hall downstairs showed no trace of yesterday. The parquet had been polished. Yellow roses, glinting with new raindrops, drooped from the rim of another Chinese bowl, filling the space with a gentle cloudy perfume. The same two mirrors examined each other, keeping silent watch. There were voices beyond the salon door, Madeleine explaining something in slow careful French.

Hearing the click of cutlery, Alex pushed at the door to the kitchen, peering inside.

John Cabot was facing him across the table, a starched linen napkin tucked neatly into his collar. He was eating an omelette with a tiny fork, pausing now and then to dab the plate with a piece of bread in his other hand. He scraped his chair back, half rising, nervously pushing the hair from his eyes.

He seemed greatly changed from those distant TPSU days. A veil of weariness had spun itself like a grey web over the familiar puffy face. Remembering the MO at Archer's ceremony, Alex wondered whether he also found his consolation in whisky.

"Alex. So here you are. I've been sitting here composing my opening sortie. Tricky thing, that ..." Running out of words, he stared uncomfortably down at his omelette.

Alex looked on, obscurely aware he had secured some kind of advantage. Somewhere in another room there was the faint sound of Justine's voice. Watching Cabot frame silent words on his lips, carefully testing them out, he was filled with an overwhelming need to be somewhere else - anywhere but here, away from this sad, desiccated man.

Cabot lurched suddenly into speech.

"Do say something, old boy, I start to feel lonely. Would you like some coffee? It's still hot. There should be a book about awkward encounters, don't you think? That translation of Apollonius Rhodius – you remember how it went? *Ill nature parted the conflicted foes* ... something like that. Are we really foes, Alex? Were we? It's a hard word. I confess I *am* a little ill-natured, but you always knew that. It's an Oxford affliction. You're not still harbouring Scottish resentments, are you? Did you never think about it from my point of view? All those months we worked together, every single operation I was tasked to perform flagged me as deniable. If you're ordered to betray your friends, how d'you think *deniable* translates? I'll tell you. *Friendless.*" He pushed his plate a little away, fragments of egg left lying there, a tiny conciliatory gesture.

"Excellent omelette. Yours is keeping warm over there. She's gone, by the way, your aunt's cook. Off to do battle. Armed to the teeth. An MP40, if I'm not mistaken. That's a dreadful thing for a girl to be toting. I hope she comes to no harm. She seemed dangerously enthusiastic."

He tried one final time, his expression a kind of sad entreaty.

"You're looking frightfully well, old chap. Better than me. The flush of success? Your mission complete ... that it?

"*Mission*? Which mission would that be, then?" Alex watched Cabot absorb his words, tuning himself to the forgotten voice, frowning slightly with the effort.

"No need to be so brusque, old man. Winners are meant to be magnanimous – isn't that the rule? Although yes, perhaps I should have said *Major Elton's* mission. He wanted you to find me. You have found me. What next?" He grinned - the same puckish expression of years ago. It was difficult not to smile back.

"I have news of the good Major, by the by. He's been moved. We found him a billet where he can do a bit less damage. He did you a fair bit, I hear. You'll be satisfied to know Major Elton's forays into amateur espionage are over. Nipped in the bud. Hats off to you for surviving his efforts. More than most would have managed. But there you are – I'm afraid his passing means you have nobody to report to."

"I can't say I care." Drawn in by the expression on Cabot's face, Alex found himself replying almost against his will. "Don't run away with the idea I was taken in by that man. The mission was misconceived from the start. I had my own reasons for going along with it."

"Your aunt started to tell me that story, but we were interrupted. I had to explain my return … my coming back. The Americans blocked the Porte d'Italie. No passage for the likes of me, at any rate. Did she explain I have a passenger? We seek refuge."

"If you think I came to Paris looking for you, you're wrong."

"No, I don't think that. You wanted to find Mrs Perry, of course you did. And you found her. All the same, I should tell you about Elton's mission. D'you know what he thought he was doing?"

"Wasn't that obvious? He was interested in you."

"Right, as ever. Can you believe it? He thought if he could only discover what I was up to, his masters would heap favours on him. Maybe promote him. I think he had a medal in mind. The snag was his masters knew perfectly well what I was up to – it was their idea, after all. But I do blame you, Alex for all that. Just a little. Apparently you gave the little chap my name. It set the poor fool thinking. Army Majors shouldn't think – it's a step too far for most of them. He was so proud of his scheme. Actually shared it with that Free French enterprise in Duke Street. Blissfully unaware that lot has been riddled with Vichy thugs since the word go. He actually invited one to your interview."

He looked up, catching Alex unawares, "But you knew all that, didn't you? How could you not?" Waiting for Alex's reluctant nod, his gaze steady. "Strange, isn't it? Wars lost because some fool wants to inhabit a bigger office. God preserve us. Just to be straight, Alex. Don't blame me for any of that. I was far away."

"Virginia, Madeleine says. Is that part of your being straight? Should I believe her?"

"Oh, yes. It's true enough. Remarkable woman, your aunt, Alex. It must run in the family. I wish I had an aunt like that. An entourage of excitable young men waving guns about. She seems to have ended up as their unofficial commandant. Mind you, what isn't unofficial these days?"

"Should I believe you? Should I believe anything you say?"

"Please yourself, old man. Believe what you will. I was in Charlottesville for almost a year. Look, this coffee's getting cold – and there's your breakfast in the oven. What's up? Don't tell me you're superstitious about breaking bread."

Alex rescued a plate from the stove, pouring himself some coffee.

Cabot sat watching him eat, leaning back, arms behind his head, suddenly confident, a comfortable expression on his face.

"Have I put an end to all your dark imaginings? I had nothing to do with the faithful Mrs P - apart from redeeming her portrait. You can imagine the flap when we got wind of that. A novel form of homicide if you think about it - putting our agents on public display. Particularly that one. I was too late, of course. I'm sorry, Alex. That's the truth – I'm really sorry. I did what I could."

"And that would be?"

"Well those two French heavies that chased her to Dundee won't be troubling anyone much ... that was a start. Detained. No don't ask where. I gather they were hauled off a train at Crewe. Of course, our Duke Street friends kicked up the hell of a fuss, kept going on about dignity, but there you are. How are we ever going to manage without emergency powers? It fell to me to tell them it was *deemed expedient*. I'd always wanted to say that."

Someone had opened the salon door, Madeleine standing in the hall asking for something, her voice too soft to make out, a darker, voice surging out, *Would you? That's kind,* the words cut off as the door clicked to.

Alex got up, walking to the door. "Perhaps we can talk later. I rather think I'm wanted. That was Justine."

"Don't go, Alex. Please don't. You'll regret it. You're not wanted there. Honestly, I know you're not. It's just woman talk. I want to tell you something. We were talking this morning, Mrs Perry and I. About Paris. About what's to become of Paris. Don't you want to know what brought me here?"

"Something to do with the Civil Administration, wasn't it? That's what Madeleine said. She painted you as a true believer, but since it's all collapsing in ruins I assume you were posted to the States to infiltrate it. To kill it off from within. That sounds more your line."

"She took so much pleasure in my gullibility ... it would have been heartless to disabuse her. But in truth we didn't need to do all that much. I think it was Mr Churchill who pointed out what a wonderful weapon we had in *misplaced enthusiasm* ... it needs English hands, of course. I offered lectures on European history. Rather a lot of them. All impromptu, I may say. You could see interest waning."

"The Americans will hardly thank you for that. Aren't they supposed to be our allies?"

"They really are endearingly naïve." It was the old Cabot again, eager face thrusting forward, eyes bright with the chase. "They can't seem to make up their mind whether they've liberated France or conquered it. Either way, they're hell bent on pulling the strings. And they don't care a damn which puppet they hang on the other end. Come on, Alex, we can't have that. For God's sake, let the frogs sort their country out. They'll bugger it up, of course, but it's theirs to bugger. Anyway - American soldiers against French politicians. I'd have said that looks like *No Contest*. It didn't need much help to come unstuck."

"It worked in Italy."

"Allied Military Government. *AMGOT*, as they insist - Americans are remarkably wedded to ugly acronyms. But they forgot about the

OT at the end. *Occupied Territories*, old boy - who's supposed to do the occupying in France? No, it was worth every bean we spent to kill that off. British perfidy at its finest ... when will people finally wake up to the fact we're good at it?"

"Aren't you running a bit ahead of yourself? A little matter of the German Garrison."

Cabot shook his head, "You were up very late, Alex. You missed the show. We stood on your little balcony, all of us, watching the cars go by. One was tempted to wave. Mercedes nose to tail. Think of all those poor bloody corporals up all night polishing. Generals in the back, dressed to the nines. A sort of gypsy caravan - bits of furniture sticking out of the boot. It says a lot – that last infantile bit of theft. Floozies at their side, of course. Admirable word, that. Your aunt used it. I gather you must be blond to qualify."

He reached out, sharing the last of the coffee pot between the two cups. "No, I never thought it possible, but your aunt will get her city back. The conquerors are off without a squeak. Top Brass first – it could start a trend."

"The place is still mined ... all the bridges ... on the Governor's orders."

Cabot looked at his watch. "In a little over an hour your new Governor is to declare a ceasefire. I heard the news last night while squabbling at the Porte d'Italie. He's to negotiate safe passage through the Swedish Consul. *Safe passage*. Prettier than *surrender*, don't you think? Von Choltitz has been busy about his reputation for days. Giving little parties, boasting that the man who flattened Sevastopol could do the same for Paris but has decided not to. He calculates he'll be forgiven. At least, forgotten. Paris is good at forgetting. He may write a book about it."

"*Negotiating*? Who with?"

"Doesn't the victor get to do that?"

"You mean the Americans?"

"Do I?"

He got up, rummaging in a coat thrown over a chair, finding a crumpled packet of cigarettes, shaking one out for Alex.

"Here, try this bit of circumstantial evidence. They're called Chesterfields. Give me a packet of Players any time."

"And this Colonel you brought back with you?"

"Our little Colonel? With your women, I think. Probably craving male company by now."

In the salon, the door to the balcony had been flung back. Puffy clouds blew across a watery sky, pale yellow sunlight slanting now and then across the breakfast table.

Madeleine was asleep, breathing damp Paris air, head lolled against the metal rail of her chair.

Justine was kneeling on the floor, one arm supporting a little boy. He had long outgrown a curious sleeveless coat fashioned from some rustic fabric. It gave him an odd clerical air. He sat on a patterned carpet, tiny legs outstretched, his head solemnly bowed over a pile of cowrie shells, slowly pushing them into piles, consumed by the intensity of play.

Hearing the salon door open, Justine looked up, her eyes alight, pressing her fingers to her lips.

# Afterword

THIS is a work of fiction. Fiction is not reality and must stand as its own truth. Readers in search of the reality of some of the events treated in this novel will find it in *Des camps dans Paris* by Jean-Marc Dreyfus and Sarah Gensburger [Librairie Arthème Fayard, 2003].

L - #0363 - 210119 - C0 - 229/152/12 - PB - DID2418666